A
Mirrored
Life

By the same author

Dozakhnama: Conversations in Hell

for dearest Brian & Ramani *August 2015*

A Mirrored Life
THE RUMI NOVEL

with love always

RABISANKAR BAL

Aruni
Shavani
Nadia &
Rumi

Translated from the Bengali by
ARUNAVA SINHA

RANDOM HOUSE INDIA

Published by Random House India in 2015
1

Copyright *Ayna Jiban* © Rabisankar Bal 2013
Translation copyright © Arunava Sinha 2015

Random House Publishers India Pvt Ltd
7th Floor, Infinity Tower C, DLF Cyber City
Gurgaon – 122002
Haryana

Random House Group Limited
20 Vauxhall Bridge Road
London SW1V 2SA
United Kingdom

978 81 8400 615 5

This book is sold subject to the condition that it shall not, by way of trade or otherwise, be lent, resold, hired out, or otherwise circulated without the publisher's prior consent in any form of binding or cover other than that in which it is published and without a similar condition including this condition being imposed on the subsequent purchaser.

Typeset in Sabon by R. Ajith Kumar

Printed and bound in India by Replika Press Private Limited

A PENGUIN RANDOM HOUSE COMPANY

Michael Madhusudan Dutt
Rabindranath Tagore
Jibanananda Das

The illuminated life of Anatolia is dedicated to these three lights of Bengal

ONE

You have not read this particular kitab of mine before, though some of you may have read my account of thirty years of travel. People refer to it as my travels now, but actually I was on a pilgrimage. Wandering from one land to another over thirty years, it struck me that there is no end to pilgrim spots on this earth; you could even say that the world itself is a place where pilgrims gather. Shaikh ibn Battuta salutes the earth and wind and air and water and fire, again and again.

Touch me if you don't believe me, I am indeed Ibn Battuta. I do have a longer name, of course. Abu Abdullah Muhammad ibn Abdullah al-Lawati al-Tanji ibn Battuta. I left Tangiers in the Hijri year 725, 1324–25 by the Christian calendar. Passing through a succession of towns, the first city I was astonished by was Alexandria. I felt I had arrived in a blue city. This was where I met Imam Burhanuddin al-Arz, from whom I heard of Maulana for the first time. The secret manuscript that I am about to read out to all of you features Maulana as its principal character. Forgive me if my idiom seems ragged rather than the language of literature. From what I have seen and understood of Maulana, he cannot be captured by the language in which books are written. Can you put the strains of a flute in words? But still I have tried, if only for myself, to create a halting narrative of this radiance. Maulana's life is like a patterned quilt. I shall be gratified if I can present even one or two of these patterns here in this majlis to all of you. Allah be merciful. All praise to the Almighty, the Keeper of the World, the Supreme Lord of Judgement Day. We pray only to you, we seek help only from you. Show us the simplest path. Show us the path of those whom you have blessed, not the path of those whom you are furious with, or of those who have lost their way.

'You want to travel in different lands, don't you?' Imam Burhanuddin asked me one day.

— Yes, such is my desire.

— When did this fancy overtake you, my friend?

— I had been to the hamam for a bath late one night. There was no one there. It was the night of the full moon, which floated in the water of the hamam. I played for a long time with the moon in the water. I've never wanted to live at home since then.

The Imam burst into laughter. — No one can stay home once the moon has struck them. Now that you *have* left, travel the world.

To tell you the truth, I had no intentions of travelling far and wide at that time. My only desire was to visit Mecca. But the Imam sahib stoked my fire. 'Off you go, then,' he said, 'Go and meet my brother Fariduddin in Hindustan. I have another brother in Sindh, Ruknuddin ibn Zakaria, and one more in China. Tell them about me.' At once I determined to visit all these places, and to take news of the Imam sahib to his brothers.

That was the beginning of thirty years of wandering. One day, I arrived in Anatolia in the course of my travels. Anatolia. The name called out to me like an evil planet. A song was concealed in it. I had also decided that I would have to visit Konya. As the Imam sahib had said, this city was the Maulana's playground. The amazing whirling dance was born here. I passed the fort at Tavas and the town of Milak to arrive at Konya. A city of water and of gardens, Konya. It rose after a cataclysmic flood, Konya. St Paul, along with Barnabas and his disciple Timothy had come here. The Christians' village conference took place here. Even after being ransacked by the Crusaders, Konya was revived as the capital of the Seljuk sultans. Not even the invasion of the Mongols could vanquish the city. And what about the people of Konya? The entire world seemed to have gathered here. Besides Turks, there were Greeks, Arabs, Indians, Iranians, Armenians, Venetians, even some Chinese. It was from this Konya that the glow of love spread to Samarqand and Bukhara. So Maulana wrote.

I heard many stories of Maulana's magical life from the Imam sahib of Alexandria. He told me, 'Maulana's poetry is written on every rock and every tree on the road to Konya. But you must discover it. And listen, examine the inns carefully. That's where the soul of Anatolia is hidden. Maulana said this world is an inn, where we wait in the depths of winter for the first day of spring, when the ice will start melting, the road will be visible, and our caravan will be on its way again.' Imam sahib used to say such strange things. One day he told me, 'Anatolia isn't just a place, another name for the soul is Anatolia.'

Anatolia got a new lease of life when the Seljuk sultan Alauddin Kayqubad ascended the throne in 1219 AD. There was a wave of construction, with new mosques, walls and inns coming up. Trade routes radiated out from Konya towards Constantinople, Aleppo, Mosul, Tabriz—and even further, to the port of Sinop on the Black Sea, to Mediterranean harbours. And countless inns came up on either side of these roads. Konya was an important centre of trade then—its only comparison could be with Baghdad. When I reached Konya sixty years after Maulana's death, it was just as lively, as full of spirit. Konya would awake to the sounds of water being splashed on the roads after the azaan at dawn. Then came the water-carriers, transporting water in goatskin bags on camelback from the canals outside the city to every home. The washermen rushed between houses to collect dirty clothes. Masons squatted by the road, waiting for work. Konya was coming alive. The lilting tones of children reading out aloud from the Quran could be heard. The fragrant vapours rising from the water suffused the hamam. Shops opened for business, deals and bargaining gathered momentum. A lunatic walked past, muttering to himself. A girl's face appeared in the window of a house, the window emptying as soon as someone's eye fell on it. Only the memory of a beauty floated about in Konya's air. All writing is actually a short-lived attempt to hold on to memory. The secret manuscript that I am about to read from is also a memory, the memory of Maulana, whom I have never seen. But how can I write about my memories of a person I have never seen? I have asked myself this question repeatedly. And a voice has asked me in return, 'Do you love Maulana?'

— Yes.

— How?

— I don't know.

— Let's say you are lost completely as you love, you do not exist anymore. Is that how you love Maulana?

— I don't know.

— Then begin, Shaikh. This ignorance will lead you to Maulana eventually. You have to move forward so that you can cook yourself.

— Cook myself?

— Do not question everything, infidel. You will understand as you write. You are the food, you are the one who eats, you are the cook.

Many years later, after I reached Tangiers on my way back home, I finished dictating the accounts of my travel to a scribe, after which I began to write Maulana's life story myself. I felt I would have to write it in my own hand, for I have heard the strains of the flute, the melody that weeps to go back home.

My learned readers, you know that there are stories even before there are stories. That is why I must first tell you about Konya. This kitab has its origins in a munaqib, a book about holy people. I must also tell you how it reached me. Unless you know this you will not be able to trust the unworthy Ibn Battuta. Moreover, I believe that before tasting a story, it is necessary to know a few things about its history and geography. For instance, the climate of the area. Unless you are aware of the weather patterns in Anatolia, much of what Maulana said would make no sense.

I was staying at a caravanserai with some merchants. The inn was named Horozluhan. There were many inns on either side of the road to Anatolia, for this was the route along which people travelled long distances for trade. Beside rooms for people, there were also arrangements for horses and camels. Even a small mosque to pray in. You had to pass through an enormous gate inlaid with intricate designs to enter the inn. I was to share a room on the first floor with three merchants. Two Arabs and one Greek, but all three knew Persian. We started talking of different things, and one of the stories I heard in the course of the conversation made a permanent spot for itself in my head. The Greek merchant told the tale. His name was Kostis Palamas. His style of storytelling was admirable, you had to hold your breath as you listened.

According to Kostis Palamas, the story was one about life's savings and expenses. Laughing, he said at one point, 'All I've done as a merchant is to save money. Now I'm waiting for a time when I can spend it.'

— A time to spend? What's that? I asked.

— The day someone in my heart tells me, spend now, spend now, spend now, Palamas.

— What will you do then?

Palamas was silent for a few minutes. Then he said, scratching his head, 'That's just what I don't know. I don't know how to spend. But I'll manage.'

— How?

— Maulana will show the way. I consider him my mentor. I have decided to become a follower of his silsilah, his religious order.

— Is this your way of spending? One of the Arab merchants asked.

Once again Palamas was silent for some time. Then he said with a smile, 'Let me tell you a qissa then. I heard it from a dervish in an inn at Aleppo. Apparently Maulana included the story in his Masnavi-e Ma'anavi.'

I am recounting the story Palamas told us. It's about a beggar named Farhad. You didn't normally see a beggar as happy as him. He would wander from one city to another. No one had ever seen the smile wiped off his face. He would always be on his way somewhere, dressed in his patched, frayed and faded clothes, and his tattered shoes. No one had ever seen him begging. He would only ask for food when he was hungry, even starving the entire day. But since there was no lack of good people on earth, he always got some food the next day. If you asked him, tell me, Farhad, what will you do when these shoes are completely worn out? How will you get another pair? Won't it hurt to walk on bare feet? Farhad would answer, 'Khuda will find me another old, torn pair. It may be a size too small or too large, but that will not prevent Farhad from moving about, huzoor.' I'm told someone once took Farhad to a shop to buy him a new pair of shoes. After the measurements had been taken, Farhad got the opportunity he was looking for and escaped. If you asked Farhad, why did you run away? he would answer, 'I don't like new shoes, they shine too much, I believe they also lead to sores on the feet, that would be very painful, my old shoes are much better. Old shoes have a warmth in them.' What warmth, Farhad? 'Don't you know? The warmth from the feet of the man who wore the shoes before me.'

It needs no special skill on my part to tell this story. I am an excellent mimic. People's gestures, the way they walk and talk, birds and beasts, the wind in the mountains, the cascading waterfalls, the flow of the river, leaves falling from trees, slithering snakes, the water boiling in the pot, the oil sizzling when something's being fried, the sound of kebabs being charred . . . I can imitate all of these. I have merely copied the way the merchant Kostis Palamas told the story. In the course of thirty years of travel from one country to another, I have come to the conclusion that there's no such thing as originality in the ways of the world. Only matter and speed are unique. May Allah protect us.

The fact is that Farhad used to trust the Imam of the mosque implicitly. Hadn't the priest told him to keep his faith in Allah always? This faith was Farhad's only resource. Trust the Lord's compassion, and you will always be taken care of, you'll see. Farhad used to float about like a current of wind. Sometimes his throat would overflow, sending torrents of music along the road. One day, when he was a long way from his own town—with no human habitation nearby, he was singing and dancing on his way—he heard a sound of weeping and mourning. Looking for the source, he came upon the Imam of the mosque, sobbing loudly beside his dog. The dog was close to dying, he would breathe his last any moment.

— What's wrong with him? Farhad asked.

Looking at him, the priest began to cry even louder. 'My dog is about to die, Farhad. How I loved him. No dog was ever so trustworthy, Farhad. He kept me company so often, guarded me all night.'

— What's the matter with him? Is he sick? Did someone attack him?

— Hunger. He was starving . . . The priest began to cry again. 'Look at him Farhad, he's gone. Gone forever. Starved to death.'

— Why?

Farhad gazed in silence at the dog. Imam sahib's pet had died of hunger? Imam sahib didn't lack for money. Why should his dog starve to death? What joke was this of Allah's? He spotted a large sack next to the priest, its mouth closed with a rope.

— What's in the sack?

— My food, the priest answered, weeping.

— Why didn't you give some to him? Farhad shouted.

— I'm going on hajj, my boy. Just imagine how far away Mecca is. I doubt if this food will be enough even for me.

— Are you human? You read sermons, but you allow your dog to starve to death.

— Consider reality, Farhad. What will I eat if my food runs out? It's a long way to Mecca.

Farhad couldn't say another word. He realized that Allah's enemy in the guise of the Imam was shedding false tears. So Farhad, what do you do now? You don't have the ability to bring the dog back to life. But say to yourself, clench your teeth and say to yourself, 'Imam sahib, you used to say that the ego is the greatest barrier to faith—one shouldn't use the word "I". You said, if you cannot love someone, Farhad, you must realize that your ego stands between the two of you. The reason that man thinks so much of the future is the ego. It was you who said over and over again, allow the "I" to go away, and you'll see that all fear and all conflict will vanish on their own. Just have faith and love, that's all you need to have Khuda on your side. But what did you do? A slice of bread was more important to you. The Lord has said, spend, spend, spend. Don't save anything. Dive like a moth into the flames of love. Try to dive in just once, Imam sahib.'

This is the qissa of the savings and expenses of life. Finishing the story, Kostis Palamas sat in silence once again. Then, rising to his feet, he said, 'Let me go and pet my horse in the stable.'

As I wandered around on my thirty years of travel, I felt that the horse is the loneliest creature in the world. A thousand times more lonely than humans. I have seen solitary horses in the field on scorching afternoons, shadowy horses have appeared in my line of sight in torrential rain. Have any of you seen a horse gazing at the full moon? To tell the truth, I have pondered so much on horses that I could have written a book about them. Have you ever wondered why the horse is the loneliest creature? I shall present a couple of theories. The horse is primarily a wild animal. Man began to tame it for personal use about four thousand years before the birth of Christ. I believe that horses are so afflicted by their memories of life in the wild that they find it impossible to avoid loneliness. At the same time they love the company of humans too. As a result they have to bear a life of so much conflict that extreme loneliness is the only outcome. I have considered this from another perspective too. The Greek god Poseidon is the god of oceans, earthquakes and horses. He crosses the seas on the back of his white steed Hippocampus. Are horses afflicted by the loneliness of the sea? Were the seeds of solitary earthquakes also planted in them? As you know, Poseidon's father was Chronos and his mother, Bea. Chronos used to eat his children as soon as they were born. It wasn't surprising that the god of time would consume his children. But when Poseidon was born his mother Bea put him away in the sheep pen. Could Poseidon not have known about his offspring-eating father? Of course he did. How deep it ran, the loneliness of one whose father had consumed all his other children. I think Poseidon's loneliness was passed on to his mount, the horse. The reason for loneliness cannot be identified scientifically. Does a person himself know when he has become lonely and why? If we cannot even tell when men become lonely, it is obviously impossible to know where the loneliness of horses springs from. For we do not have even a smattering of the language of horses. I see innumerable horses, white and black and brown, floating away through an infinite emptiness, I hear their cries piercing the horizons, there they are, galloping, they appear like marooned pedestrians in space.

Forgive me, I am being snared in a web of my own words. I must return to the original subject. But do you know what is real and what is a copy, Ibn Battuta? I am about to tell you about the lives of the shadows that appeared on the walls of the cave referred to by Aflatoon, whom all of you know as the noble Plato. These shadows are a lie, and yet they are the truth too. This story shall proceed towards its destiny through a game of noughts and crosses between truth and falsehood. Shaikh Ibn Battuta believes that all stories in the world are bound by fate.

So, what happened was that some people came to meet me the next morning. All of them were members of the Futuwwa. The Futuwwa was not just an organization, it was also an ideology for reaching moral heights through compassion. I accepted the hospitality of many such Futuwwas in Turkman cities. They comprised Sufi monks, merchants and artisans. The idea of the Futuwwa was brought to Anatolia by Umar-al Suhrawardi, the principal advisor to Al-Nasir, the Abbasid Caliph. He even wrote a book about the principles of the Tokat-e al-Nasiri Futuwwa in 1290. It said that the Futuwwa is one of the levels on the way to uniting with Allah. Those who did not have the qualities necessary to lose themselves in the Lord through the annihilation of the ego, Fana fi-Allah, could at least go as far as the Futuwwa to sense him. The head of a Futuwwa was known as the Akhi, meaning brother, and his disciples were the Fityan, or young men. The place where they stayed was known as a Jawaiya—the Dervish Inn. I even saw some Futuwwas with two or three Akhis, under whom groups of Fityan worshipped in silence. The Fityan were primarily merchants and artisans. They worked all day at their business and their craft to make a living, and then found their happiness in serving guests all evening. No matter where a traveller came from, what kind of person they were, or what their religion was, everyone was equal at Dervish Inn. Whenever a member of the Futuwwa heard of the arrival of a guest to their city, they sought out this guest. This was how Qazi Ibn Kalam Shah came to meet me at the inn with his band of young men. They were dressed in khirqas, or patchwork robes.

Kissing my hand, Qazi Ibn Kalam told me, 'As long as you are in Konya, Shaikh, you must stay at our Futuwwa. You mustn't say no.'

— But I'm comfortable at this serai.

— You're a guest of this city, Shaikh. We won't receive Allah's mercy unless we are given the chance to look after you.

Putting his hand on my back, Kostis Palamas said, 'Pack your bags, Shaikh, unless you visit the Futuwwa you'll never know how noble hospitality can be.'

— Maulana's house was always filled with people. Gripping my hand, Qazi Ibn Kalam continued, 'Maulana would say, how will you serve your guest unless he visits you at home? You will reach him, Al-Kabir, through hospitality to your guest.'

Turning to my companions, I said, 'Then all of you must come too.'

— We're leaving in a short while, Shaikh. The horses are feeding, as soon as they're done . . .

— Aren't you going to explore Konya? I asked.

One of the Arab merchants said miserably, 'We've come to—and left—Konya so many times. But we haven't had the chance to explore. It's not in our fate, Shaikh. The demands of business are very selfish.'

Qazi Ibn Kalam said, 'Why not stay back in Konya? You see these young men, they're the Fityan from our Futuwwa, but many of them are actually merchants. Even traders have to think of the Lord.'

The Qazi's young men packed my belongings without allowing me to help.

Palamas walked me up to the gate of the caravanserai. When I said goodbye, he put his hand on my shoulder and said, 'We shall meet again, Shaikh.'

— Where? I smiled. — I shall wait.

— Here, in this very Konya.

— How?

— I decided last night. I shall move here and join the Fityan in one of the Futuwwas.

— When?

— It will take a year or so.

— But I won't be here then. I'll have to leave too. Hindustan, Sinhala, China, Espanha . . . I must visit these places.

Palamas was silent for some time. Then he took a tiny mirror from the pocket of his coat and handed it to me.

— Keep this, Shaikh.

— Why?

— I've noticed that you haven't a mirror of your own.

— But I can see my reflection in a hundred different places. In shops, at inns, at the barber's.

Palamas smiled. — That's like looking at yourself in the marketplace. You're going to be travelling a long way, you'll visit so many different places, you'll see and hear so many different things, and as you go through all these experiences, I am certain that you will grow more beautiful, more pure. Take a look at yourself then.

— Why?

— Let me tell you a story. Maulana wrote it in his Masnavi. You know of Joseph, the man of God. No man more beautiful has ever been born on earth, or ever will be. One day a friend was visiting him. 'What gift have you brought me?' asked Joseph. Shrinking back in shame, the friend said, 'You lack for neither beauty nor wealth. I thought hard about what to bring you, but there was nothing I could think of. Whatever I give you cannot be anything more than a drop in the ocean. So I have brought you a lovely mirror. Even the sun is jealous of you. You can see your beauty in this mirror, nothing could be more beautiful.'

Smiling, I said, 'I am not Joseph.'
— I am fortunate that I could give you this mirror.
— Why?
— In my head it is Joseph I am giving it to.

TWO

The Caliph Ghazi Dervish Inn. A building surrounded by gardens at a distance from the city. Currents of water as clear as crystal flowed around the inn, with snow white swans swimming in them. Columns of water rose skywards from fountains in the sky, arcing outwards like petals. Swarms of cranes waded in the water. Many of the people I had met on the way had told me that it was a matter of great fortune to live in Konya in the springtime. The city turned into a second paradise in this season. One of the primary subjects of Maulana's poetry was spring. He sang praises to the season in many different ways. The sun was at the centre of his imagination. In spring the sun enters Aries, distributing new life across the world. Roses bloom, there is a celebration of green everywhere, and the streets are perfumed with the fragrance of oleaster trees. Resembling the willow, this tree has unusual yellow flowers. The Caliph Ghazi Dervish Inn was also redolent with the sharp scent of the oleaster. We shall have more to say about spring later, for it is impossible to reach

Maulana's soul without this season.

Sometimes, after the young men at the inn had left on their respective businesses after the early-morning namaz, Qazi Ibn Kalam and I conversed as we strolled in the garden. He told me about the devotion needed for a Sufi life, and the different routes that devotees take, but Maulana was woven into every single thing he said. One day, I asked him, 'What did Maulana look like?'

— I have never seen him, Shaikh. But I have heard stories.

— Who told you?

— Many who have seen him. Maulana was tall, thin, pale. His beard was grey, his eyebrows were bushy and his eyes were reddish brown. It seems he was very embarrassed one day to see his own reflection while bathing at the hamam. Later he said, I have caused so much suffering to this body given by Allah. Apparently he was underweight, because of long periods of fasting. I'm told he used to eat once in three days, sometimes even once a week. It's a mystery how he survived.

— On my travels I have heard of many holy men in Hindustan, Qazi sahib. It seems they meditate in the Himalayan mountains without food for years on end.

— How is that possible, Shaikh?

— How much do we know of what is possible and what isn't, Qazi sahib?

— I believe Maulana would say, 'I have no appearance, no colour. When I cannot see myself, how can you expect to see me? I am nothing but a solitary mirror.' Let me tell you a story, Shaikh. It's from Maulana's own life. Parwana Moinuddin Sulaiman's wife Gurcu Khatun was Maulana's disciple. It was Moinuddin Sulaiman who actually ruled Konya on behalf of Sultan Ruknuddin. One day Gurcu Khatun desired to have a portrait of Maulana painted. The artist arrived. 'Come,' smiled Maulana. 'Paint me if you can.' When he completed his portrait, the artist turned to Maulana to discover a face completely different from the one he had just painted. He started afresh. After he was done, he looked at Maulana only to see yet another face. When this had happened several times, the artist put down his palette. That was when Maulana said, 'I have no appearance, no colour. Considering I cannot even see myself, how can you expect to see me?'

— Amazing.

— Indeed. I cannot grasp the idea.

Qazi Ibn Kalam was lost in deep thought. He detached himself from me and began to walk about the garden by himself.

I seldom confined myself to the inn. I preferred to roam the streets of Konya. The fact is that spending too much time indoors or within a limited space makes me choke. There is no friend more intimate than the road. It's the kind of friendship that holds back nothing, only taking you from one mystery of life to another.

Take this city, Konya. The more I explored it, the more I felt its mysteries will never end. The enigma of any city is most obvious in its markets. Let me tell you about Konya's market. It's a bustling place from early in the morning to late at night. Walking along the lane running past the goldsmiths' shops, you hear the rhythmic, metallic sound of gold plates being hammered. The sound keeps ringing in your head. This is where Salauddin the goldsmith had his shop. It was while walking along this path that Maulana had suddenly discovered Salauddin, the uneducated artisan who became his favourite friend and follower. After the goldsmiths, it's the turn of carpet merchants and needlework artists. Most of the carpets come from Damascus or Silesia. The needlework shops are small, the artists doing their work on the spot, bringing intricate patterns to life in different colours, the swift piercing movements of their needles giving birth to creepers and flowers and birds. One of the artists told me that Maulana had apparently wanted an embroidered cover for Buraq's saddle, made with his own blood and tears.

The bookshops are like an art gallery. Each book is a painting. Qurans in hundreds of forms, each one more beautiful than the next. The smallest of the Qurans can be concealed within a fist. Silver muhafazas or boxes with decorative designs are available to store these tiny Qurans. How soft the velvet boxes are. The tapestries hung on the walls are mesmerizing, each of them a breathtaking universe of artistry depicting a saying from the Quran or the Hadith.

The perfumeries are shishmahals. Their walls are covered in mirrors, while rows of shelves are stacked with vials of ittar in different colours. Pouring a drop or two on their fingertips, the shopkeepers rub them on your wrist, enough to make your entire body fragrant. One of the perfumers told me about the mystery of scents. Why are we overcome by them? Pleasant scents take us to the distant past, arousing memories of our happiness in the company of the most loved persons in our life.

The fragrance is not limited to the perfumes. There's the aroma of a variety of kebabs, venison, lamb, and a profusion of sweets. The smells are intoxicating. The kofte iskender kebab and the alti izmeni kebabs vary in taste and flavour. The taboos seekh kebab melts in the mouth like butter. And why not? Turkey meat is marinated for a long time in a mixture of milk, onions, olive oil, tomato juice, salt, and pepper. The arabasi is a delicious soup made with turkey, while the caskek is made with a shoulder of lamb. Its taste is unparalleled. The karniyarik doesn't lag behind either. Succulent eggplant stuffed with minced lamb. Vinegar-marinated venison coated with spices and grilled on skewers, its taste unfurling its wings slowly. A memorable sweetmeat made with almond paste and pomegranate seeds. It's a variety of halva. And is there anyone who isn't aware of Konya's famous halvas? Let me tell you a little about irmik halva. The butter must be heated on a low flame without salt. When bubbles appear, the farina, a flour of ground wheat or barley, must be fried in it. Now add water and sugar and deep-fry it.

One of the sweets has a startling name—hanim gobegi, meaning, a lady's navel. I must mention the baclava too.

Thin layers of flour fried in butter, with sliced nuts and honey deep in the centre. I have to return to food and cooking later. Some of the principal themes of Maulana's devotion and poetry are accompaniments to cooking. All that is raw must be made delicious and digestible through the process of cooking. The Lord will cook you with his own hands, for only then can he savour you.

Sometimes I go to the enormous mosque located on top of a hill a short way from the city. Sultan Alauddin Kayqubad had built this mosque in the year 1221 AD. Its exterior is unadorned, but inside, the minbar of expensive wood, the pulpit from which the Maulvi sahib delivers the khutba, the Friday sermon, is laid out in an extraordinary geometric pattern. The eyes are drawn to the semi-circular mihrab, the niche indicating the direction of Mecca, whose beauty lies in its fine inscriptions in which Allah's names are written in patterns of sky-blue, black and white tiles. This mihrab is luminescent with the uniqueness of Seljuk art. Maulana would come here to read the afternoon namaz on Fridays. Qazi Ibn Kalam told me that Maulana wrote in his divan:

> All my praying has turned me into a prayer
> Anyone who sees me only wants prayer as alms

Descending from the hill, I stand in front of the Karata Madrassa. A small domed building. Maulana's friend Wazir Jalaluddin had founded this madrassa in 1251 AD in Karata for studies in natural science. The most beautiful names of Allah are inscribed in Arabic on the stone. The interiors are astounding. The dome is covered with a pattern of stars, an uncountable number of them, all linked to one another. The observatory had been constructed with the same sky-blue, black, and white tiles. I'm told that the patterns of stars cannot be deciphered without higher mathematics, and once they are deciphered, the positions of the stars in the sky can be calculated too.

Walking on, I stop at Sadruddin Kunai's tomb. This adopted son of Ibn Arabi was the greatest interpreter of his father's philosophy. Maulana and Sadruddin were contemporaries. Maulana's path was the one of love, while Sadruddin trod the path of knowledge. Sadruddin used to be suspicious of Maulana once, but the mistrust was wiped out afterwards. Sufis often argue about which of them was greater: Ibn Arabi or Maulana. But they travelled on different roads, one leading to learning and the other, to passion. The sun of Maulana's life, Shams Tabrizi, had once told him, 'If you are a pearl, Ibn Arabi is nothing but a pebble.'

Maulana's house in Konya is in ruins now. Only homeless pigeons fly around it. With the fluttering of their wings and their cooing ringing in my ears, I approach Maulana's grave. Engraved with calligraphy and patterns, the tombstone is soiled out of neglect. Someone told me, come instead to the garden of Meram by the river, Shaikh. Hailing a horse-drawn carriage, I climbed in. The coachman was twenty-four or twenty-five at most. 'How long have you been driving a carriage?' I asked him.

— Ten years, huzoor.
— You started very young.
— It was a severe winter that year. Everything covered in ice. A powdery snow kept falling incessantly from the skies. Abba died, and with his death, I was yoked to the carriage.

Meram. A dream laid out on the slopes of hills. A garden made by Allah himself. A stream flowing along. I've heard that Maulana often sat down on its banks with his disciples, filling the air with music and conversation. Distracted by the sounds of the currents and whirlpools, he would walk about aimlessly, while lines from his poetry were borne away by the wind.

The young coachman sat in silence at my side by the river.

— What's your name?
— Mujib, huzoor.
— Do you know how many names Allah has?

Mujib scratched his head. Placing my hand on his shoulder, I told him, 'You're named after Allah.'

He looked at me with wide eyes. — Really, huzoor?
— One of Allah's names is Mujib. Allah has ninety-nine names, Mujib.
— So many names for just one man? He laughed in astonishment.
— The most beautiful names are all his. Do you read the namaz?
— I do.
— Read it now.

— It's not time for the namaz, huzoor.
— You're right. How do you read it? Loudly or softly?
— Loudly, huzoor.
— Never read it loudly. Nor softly. Read it in a middle voice.
— Very well.
— In life the middle path is preferable, Mujib.

He stared at me uncomprehendingly. I realized that this forest and stream in Meram had drawn me into a dream. Why was I telling a young man of twenty-five all this? Why would he even understand? But I felt that Mujib had to understand. He had been born in Konya, and Maulana had been born here too. Mujib had to bear the burden of history. His birthplace had given him this responsibility. A homeless man on a road in Espanha had once told me, history is not an event or a story, history is an obligation, which you are compelled to bear during your human existence.

The Caliph Ghazi Inn woke up when evening fell. One by one, the young men returned from their day's work. Every night, one of the Fityan was assigned the responsibility of fetching the requirements for dinner. The cooking proceeded with great zest in the kitchen. And Qazi Ibn Kalam busied himself completing the Halqa. Zikr, or uttering the names of Allah, is an essential task in Sufi worship. Repeating one, or all ninety-nine, of Allah's names continuously is known as the Zikr, and a collective Zikr, as the Halqa-e Zikr. The voice and the body are both intoxicated by Allah's names, which Sufis refer to as Zikr-e Zehri.

Even after reading the namaz five times, the worship of Allah remains incomplete to Sufis without the night-time prayer, the Tahajjud. The Quran says, 'Pray at night but do not pray all night.' So Qazi Ibn Kalam had to keep an eye on everything—whether the young men had bathed properly and dressed appropriately, whether the area where they sat for the Zikr had been cleaned, whether enough rose essence had been sprinkled to attract the angels and nymphs. Qazi examined it all personally. He would tell me, 'What a predicament Allah has placed me in, Shaikh! I pray for darkness all day, the way the shepherd calls out to his flock. I call out to the darkness the way birds search for their nests at sunset. When the darkness spreads and others fall asleep, that's when we awaken, turning our eyes towards Khuda-tallah to talk to him. The Zikr is nothing but a conversation with the Lord while uttering his names.'

The Halqa-e Zikr continued. The rise and fall of the concerted waves of voice and body. Allahu Akbar, Allahu Akbar . . . I watched from my place. At one point it felt as though the prayer room was flying through space. Just like the birds in the compositions of Fariduddin Attar of Nishapur, who flew behind the hoopoe, the bird of knowledge, towards Mount Qaf. What I heard was not human utterance but the sound of wings. I flew along with them. Someone said from afar, 'Come back to earth, Shaikh. You must travel on foot, flight is not for you. You have to walk to all the places you want to visit, see all you want to see. The birth of man, his death, his becoming god and the devil. You must walk and you must observe, Shaikh, this form of devotion is not for you.'

— Why not?

— You are here to write of the itinerant life, Shaikh. No one can write once they have accomplished their mission.

— Why not?

— These letters, and then words, and then sentences, that are written on your manuscript are all answers to questions. Writing is nothing but a long journey of confronting questions. Accomplishment will bring you peace, but will not make a writer of you. This peace and union together is fana, the annihilation of self. Which do you want, Shaikh? Fana, or to write?

— To write.

— Why do you want it?

— Writing is magical. It remains, and it vanishes. I want both of these.

Every night I fell asleep during the Halqa, only to be woken up by Ibn Kalam.

— Why do you fall asleep every night, Shaikh? Qazi asked me.

— This Zikr transports me somewhere, I don't know where . . .

— Why don't you join us? The Zikr unburdens both the mind and the body.

Smiling, I told him, 'This is not my path, Qazi sahib.'

— Why not?

— I have a long way to go. I shall not go back home till

I have seen much, much more.

— But you will have to go back home one day, Shaikh.

— When?

— No one but Allah knows . . .

Qazi Ibn Kalam set out with me that night.

— Where are we going?

— To hear the flute. In Meram.

— At this hour of the night?

— We'll get a carriage. Don't worry. It's Friday. A mystic visits Meram on Friday nights to play the flute.

— Whom does he play for?

— For Maulana.

We heard the strains of the flute as soon as we reached Meram. Like a torrent of teardrops rending the sky apart. I felt as though we were not on earth but floating in space, flailing about in a cosmic current of incessant weeping. When we reached the river I shouted, 'Tell him to stop, Qazi sahib, I cannot bear such sadness.'

The dervish stopped playing the flute and burst out laughing. Coughing between gusts of laughter, he said, 'You are a flute too, my son. Do you remember the forest of reeds from which you were sliced off?'

— No, Maulana.

— There is only one Maulana. We are all his disciples. Can you hear the weeping within yourself? Do you know why the flute weeps?

Without waiting for an answer, the dervish began to play his flute again. When I woke up in the morning, Meram was deserted. Neither Qazi nor the mystic was present. The waters of the stream were flowing over my feet.

When I returned to the Dervish Inn, Qazi Ibn Kalam embraced me.

— Where were you all night, Shaikh?

— Why, don't you know where I was?

— I looked for you all night.

— But you . . .

— I what?

— You took me to Meram to listen to the dervish playing the flute.

— Me?

— Don't you remember?

Smiling, Qazi said, 'Go to bed now, Shaikh. Sleep through the day.'

— Why?

— You listened to the flute all night. Do you know why the flute weeps?

— It wants to return to the wood of reeds from which it was taken.

Qazi embraced me again. — I will take you to a calligraphist tomorrow.

— Will it be you or someone else? I asked, smiling.

— That's true, I have no idea who took you there last night. But tomorrow it will be me. You will leave soon. If the book can be completed before you go . . .

— What book?

— The novel about Maulana that Yaqut al-Mustasimi is writing. You can take the manuscript with you.

THREE

Several lanes had to be crossed to reach Yaqut al-Mustasimi's workshop. Everyone called it Al-Mustasimi's adabistan, home of books, abode of literature. A dark staircase led to an enormous hall on the first floor, with innumerable doors and windows. Just outside lay fields of grain, with the hills beyond them. Mustasimi's adabistan was on the edge of Konya. I believe his book-making workshop was at the heart of the city once upon a time. But as Mustasimi grew older, he began to look for a location near fields and mountains. A merchant who came to know of this donated this house to Mustasimi. Walking through the lanes leading to the workshop, I could not have imagined the wondrous luminescence that awaited me. Before entering the hall, I stood in the balcony to admire the exquisite design of nature, the green fields and the grim mountains, while clouds clustered in the sky. Someone whispered in my ear, look at this, Shaikh, look at this incomparably beautiful dance, which has never begun, which will never end.

Dance, dance in your blood, Maulana had written in one of his poems.

With his shoulder-length white hair and white beard, Al-Mustasimi resembled an angel. His robe was a patchwork of different colours. He stooped with age, and his vision was blurred. Qazi Ibn Kalam had told me that he had personally written more than a thousand copies of the Quran. Al-Mustasimi ran his adabistan with about forty students. Some of them wrote, some illustrated, and many of them were involved in book-binding.

His chamber of pen and ink was fragrant with the scent of ittar. The Lord lived in this room, writing our lives with his pen. Sometimes his pen and ours merge. We copy this noble calligraphist when we write for ourselves. Time can never erase what the pen writes. Al-Mustasimi had told me later, 'Remember this, Shaikh, calligraphy is divine geometry. To master this geometry the pupil must first study the teacher's calligraphy with close attention, taking it into his eyes. We call this phase of learning the art of calligraphy nazari. Then comes the kalami, when identical copies of the calligraphy must be made with quills. It is a prolonged apprenticeship. Only then can the real calligraphist emerge, when he qualifies for the ikazet, the authorization to actually write a book.'

The scratches of pens running over paper could be heard in the adabistan. So many hues in the ink pots—black, scarlet, the sheen of gold, the calm beauty of the colour extracted from sapphires. On the other side of the hall books were being bound. I was drunk on the smell of ink, pens and glue. I felt as though I had been born of the agony of writing a single letter, in a room just like this where calligraphy was practised.

Learning who I was, Al-Mustasimi gripped my hand tightly, saying, 'So you are out to conquer the world, Shaikh?'

— You think I am capable of such a feat? Sultans conquer the world.

— Never mind the sultans. Do you suppose the world can be conquered by killing people? Maulana had written:

I am so small, barely visible
How can I bear such deep love?
Look at your eyes. So small,
Yet how large the things they see.

It is with these eyes that you have gone out into Khudatallah's world, Shaikh. I envy your fortune. And my life has passed copying manuscripts in a tiny room.

— You have seen the world through your books. You have seen the world in a grain of sand.

— I don't know. But living amongst these pens and ink and manuscripts, I feel he lives in my adabistan.

— He is indeed here, janab.

— You believe that? Al-Mustasimi looked at me, his eyes misty.

— He invented the pen first, then the ink pot.

— Tell us, Shaikh, tell us how we were born.

— Using the ink from the ink pot he wrote about us.

— And we were born. Trembling, Al-Mustasimi rose to his feet. — We came into being from his pen, every single book.

Some of Al-Mustasimi's students surrounded him.

— Calm down, huzoor.

— Give me a pen, let me write Bismillah's name.

The quill seemed to fly like a bird as Al-Mustasimi started writing on a sheet of white paper.

When he had finished he handed it to me. — Keep this with you all the time as you travel the world, Shaikh. He, the stork, will take you back home again. This life of ours is actually a tale of homecoming.

— I wonder when I'll return . . .

— I'm not talking of your birthplace. That's not your home. The question is, when will you return to Khuda's pen, to the ink pot . . . Ha ha ha . . .

Suddenly Qazi Ibn Kalam asked, 'How far are you from finishing your own book?'

— My own book?

— The Masnavi you're writing about Maulana.

Laughing, Al-Mustasimi said, 'Really, Qazi sahib, do you think there's anything like one's own book? All this time that I've spent writing the Quran—is it not my own book? I have tried to write each and every Quran as beautifully as I can. If you ever examined the books, Qazi sahib, you'd see that I have tried to discover the Lord afresh in every Quran I have written.'

— How did you try to find him anew? Qazi Ibn Kalam frowned.

— I shan't argue, Qazi sahib. Al-Mustasimi stopped smiling.

— Just asking. Qazi smiled.

— You will know for yourself one day. Let me tell you what you wanted to know. It'll take some more time to complete the Masnavi about Maulana. As you realize, I can barely see. But what use will it be to you?

— I was thinking, if the Shaikh were to take it around the world . . .

— Then I'll have to make a copy.

— I'm sure one of your students here can do it quickly.

— That's true. Al-Mustasimi trained his dull eyes on me again. — Do you really want to take it with you, Shaikh?

— I do.

After a pause, Al-Mustasimi said, 'Then you'll have to spend a few days in my adabistan. And while you're here I shall tell you incredible stories.'

— I'm ready, I told him excitedly.

— You'll stay in my guest chamber. You'll be very comfortable. Kimia knows how to take care of guests.

— Who's Kimia?

— My daughter. Khuda had left her on the road for me. Nothing but a virgin sheet of paper. She's turning into a book now. A real book of the heart. Dilkitab.

Al-Mustasimi's guest chamber was a small room on the second-floor terrace. I moved from the Caliph Dervish Inn to his well-appointed little room. Standing on the terrace made me want to fly over the fields of grain towards the mountains. A song floated in from somewhere in a language from the future of a faraway land I did not understand: 'Why was the sky trembling, why was the ground dancing.'

Al-Mustasimi told me, 'I will come to your ibadat khanah after the evening namaz every day.'

— You have given me this house of worship yourself, janab.

— Who am I to give anything, Shaikh? I'd been looking for a place like this for years. It was the Lord who made sure I got it. You cannot sit in the middle of the town and write books. You must see the greenery now and then, the mountains from time to time. You become one with the grains in the field, and you put your arms around the mountains so that you can disappear in the distance. How can you get your pen strokes right without this? That's why I was seeking such a place like a mad dog. As they say, your worship will fail if you fritter away your time. You will see the fields of grain by day of course, Shaikh, but you must stay awake one night to feel the mountains. Oh the wind that blows on the mountain peak—it will make you feel as though a storm is battering the doors of your heart.

The work of writing and illustrating books began early in the morning at Al-Mustasimi's adabistan. The next morning I told him, 'I want to learn the art of writing books while I'm here, janab.'

— What use is it for you? You'll never write a book.

— No harm learning.

Al-Mustasimi smiled. — Don't try to master every

art, Shaikh. Observe, listen. But make your wish to your mentor only for the path that is yours. You'd better go with Kimia instead.

— Go where?

— To the mountain. Kimia takes the sheep out to graze every day. Walk around with them, Shaikh. Kimia plays the flute very well, too.

I had seen Kimia already the previous night. She had brought my dinner to my room. I don't know how to describe her. I have heard many dervishes speak of the full moon on a moonless night. A dark-skinned girl—I was sure the foundling Kimia had Moorish blood, for her eyes were like an arrow strung up in a bow; she had a generous forehead, a prominent nose, thick lips, and long arms. She moved as swiftly as a deer in the wild. Most of all I liked it when she laughed, for she often turned into a waterfall of laughter.

I would go out with Kimia every morning. She would drive the sheep along a path cutting through the heart of the fields towards the mountain, and I would follow, running when I fell out of rhythm with her. Grazing on the grass and foliage, the sheep would wander high up the hillside, white dots and stars from a distance. Once the sheep had been let loose Kimia and I would sit by a waterfall. Kimia would bring food for both of us. She talked incessantly. I felt that her unending conversation was not with me but with herself. She played the flute whenever the fancy took her. I remained sitting, looking at the moon on a moonless night.

My days passed with Kimia on the mountain and listening to the nearly blind Al-Mustasimi tell stories in the evening. In the isolation of the mountain, amidst the sounds of the waterfall coursing down, touching the rocks, I did not even realize when Kimia and I discovered each other's bodies. One day Kimia asked me, 'Will you take me with you?'

— Take you where?
— Wherever you go.

For a long time I couldn't answer. Then I said, 'I will, Kimia. I will.'

FOUR

Welcome, Shaikh. Our stories start this evening. Pray to the Lord to keep us safe while we tell this story, may it cover us like a shroud in our graves too. Remember, there are many tales in these verses. The stories and poems move about in the earth and sky and wind and space like pollen grains. I will tell you the story of a dervish's life. Some people say the title of this story is *Bagh-o Bahar. The Garden and Spring*. How will you reach Maulana's life without crossing the garden and the spring, Shaikh? The spring is nothing but the Messiah, Jesus Christ, who gives new life to dead trees. Listen to what Maulana is saying, everyone has eaten their dinner and gone to bed. The house is absolutely empty. Come, let us go into the garden, so that the apples can consort with the peaches. We will bear messages between the roses and the magnolias. Christ is spring, he removes the shroud covering dead plants to awaken them. In gratitude their lips part, they want kisses. Do you know why the rose and the tulip are burning? There's a flame within them.

As we weave the tale of the dervish it is this flame in whose search our journey begins, Shaikh. Now for the story. Azad Bakht was the Sultan of Turkistan at the time. Don't ask which year it was. Time in a story is an endless flow, with neither a beginning nor an ending. The Sultan's capital was Constantinople. There was unlimited wealth in the treasury, and everyone was happy with the Sultan's administration. There was no theft, no robbery; the doors of houses and shops weren't even locked at night.

Sultan Azad Bakht was a god-fearing man. There was both happiness and peace in the kingdom, but his only regret was not having a son. After offering the namaz five times a day, he would constantly pray to Allah for a male child. As you can imagine, Shaikh, the palace appeared dark to him without a son. Who would preserve his lineage after his death, who would occupy the throne? He was a ruler by nature, after all—despite being god-fearing he never lost his sense of entitlement. But then, it was also true that the Lord had made him the Sultan, and it was he who had given him his rights. Nothing is possible unless Allah wills it. Who are we to judge?

The Sultan had just passed forty. Walking around in the shishmahal one day, he stopped abruptly on seeing himself in a mirror. Do you know what he saw? A single white hair in his beard, glittering like silver. A sigh emerged. Looking at his own reflection, he muttered, 'What have I achieved in this life, my Lord? What will I do with this huge Sultanate and all this gold and jewels? The Day of Judgement is not far. A male heir is not in my destiny.

There's no one to leave all this to.'

The Sultan decided to forsake his realm and spend his remaining days praying to Khuda. He told his prime minister and other ministers to look after the kingdom now and not disturb him anymore. His days passed in fasting and praying. There was no one who dared request him to return from his self-imposed exile.

As soon as the news of the Sultan's abdication spread, trouble began to brew. Scoundrels became active, and revolts and riots erupted across the kingdom. You could say that a peaceful state was swallowed by anarchy. But who was willing to inform the Sultan of all this and ask him to return to the task of administration? After consultations, the ministers appeared at the door of the oldest prime minister, Khiradmand.

— If things go on this way the kingdom will be destroyed, Wazir-e Azam.

After some thought, Khiradmand said, 'Then come, let us all go together. I hope he will not turn down our prayer.'

The Sultan did not allow anyone but Khiradmand to enter his chamber. This old man had contributed in no small measure to the expansion of his kingdom.

Khiradmand found the Sultan looking gaunt and pale, his eyes sunken. He had served the Sultan and even his father for many years. Weeping at the Sultan's appearance, the old man crumpled at his feet. — Why did I not die before seeing you in this state, janab? What sin have I committed to be subjected to this sight?

Helping the old man to his feet, the Sultan said, 'You're

pleased to see me, aren't you? Now please leave me alone.'

Holding his hand, Khiradmand said through his tears, 'Just answer one question, janab.'

— What is it?

— Why did you withdraw this way, janab?

— What's wrong with that?

— The Sultanate is no longer as it used to be, janab. The big fish are eating the small fish, and themselves being eaten by bigger fish. Think about the hard work that your ancestors had to do to build this kingdom. Is it right to let it be destroyed? Why did you have to take this decision? What ails you? Your servant is ready to do anything for you.

— I know, Khiradmand, that you can even lay down your life for me. But there is no one who can help me today.

— Why not, janab?

— I don't have the language to convey the deep sorrow that pervades my heart. The important thing is that I'm getting older, and Judgement Day is not far away.

— You are in your youth compared to my age, janab.

— I have no son, Khiradmand. Who will succeed me, then? No one can understand this pain. That is why I have withdrawn. I am no longer interested in this Sultanate.

— What are you saying, huzoor?

— Yes, Khiradmand, I want to go away to a desolate mountain somewhere. I shall spend the rest of my days there in the service of the Lord. I want to stand before him with a pure heart on Judgement Day, Khiradmand.

— Have faith in Khuda, janab.

— Will he give me a son? The Sultan gripped Khiradmand's arm tightly. — Will Allah be kind to me?

— What can I tell huzoor that he doesn't know already? He created eighteen thousand worlds by uttering a single word, and you think he can't give you a son? My request to you is that you assume all your responsibilities once more, or else the kingdom will be destroyed. Pardon my insolence, but you will have to answer for this on Judgement Day otherwise. And all the prayers that you have sent up to the Lord will be of no use either.

— Why not? The Sultan's eyes looked even more sorrowful.

— You say you want to go away to the mountains. Is this what a Sultan should be doing? The Lord has given him other tasks, huzoor. The Sultan will rule over his kingdom and ensure everyone's welfare. That's what you have been doing all this while. It is the Lord's wish that you perform the duties of the Sultan. You must always keep Khuda in your mind, but you must complete the tasks he has assigned to you. Keep your faith in him. He is certain to give you what you want.

The Sultan sat in silence for a long time. Then he said, 'Tell all the ministers to come tomorrow.'

Khiradmand almost started dancing. — As long as this world and paradise are in existence, huzoor, so is your throne.

Peace returned to the Sultan's kingdom.

— I've heard this story somewhere, I said.

'Entirely possible,' smiled Al-Mustasimi. 'Stories often

move from one place to another, Shaikh. But you do know, don't you, that all old stories become new again?'

— How, janab?

— Let's say a story from Konya reaches Damascus. Now it starts living a different life in Damascus. The story has a new wife, new children. It is no longer a story from Konya. But still it can be recognized, do you know why? By its eyes. Wherever you go, no matter how much you change, the language of your eyes will remain unaltered. Then why should the language of a story's eyes change, janab?

— How strange. The eyes of a story?

— Stories look at people. What do they look with? Eyes, of course.

— What did the Sultan do then?

— His kingdom ran smoothly. One day, while reading a book, the Sultan came across some striking lines.

— What were they?

— O agonized, helpless man, surrender yourself to the Lord. Go to the cemetery and pray to him. Never forget that you are nothing compared to him. Remember that many powerful sultans and navabs have been born in this world and left it too, there is no sign of them even in the dust anymore. No one knows of them. You are a mere actor in a puppet show.

— And then?

— One night the Sultan left the palace in disguise without informing anyone. He walked to the graveyard outside the city. A terrible storm sprang up. The violent wind swept up everything in its path. But the Sultan did not attempt to return. He could see a flame in the distance, unwavering despite the storm. Who had ever seen such a miraculous sight? The Sultan walked on. Near the flame, he discovered four dervishes sitting with their heads tucked between their knees. Their bodies were trembling. Other than this occasional quivering, they seemed to be dead. Suddenly the Sultan felt that these four fakirs were there to pray to Allah on his behalf, and that he was bound to sire a son. The very next moment, though, he was wracked by doubt.

— Why?

— What if they were the devil's followers?

— What happened after that, janab?

— The Sultan hid himself near the fakirs, so as to watch them and listen to them. The place was empty except for the roaring of the wind, which was deeper than silence. One of the fakirs sent up a Zikr, 'Allahu Akbar!' The other three dervishes raised their heads to look at him. Then they all fell silent again. Lighting hookahs, they waved the smoke away.

— And the Sultan?

— He wasn't a Sultan anymore, Shaikh, just an observer. Such is the Lord's might, he can turn a sultan into a worm.

— And then?

— One of the dervishes said, 'Friends, we have witnessed many ups and downs in life, travelled a great deal. We don't even know one another. And yet tonight the four of us are sitting here together. None of us knows what tomorrow will bring. We have to spend the night together. I have a proposal.

— What is it? One of the others asked.
— Can't we tell one another the stories of our long lives? We can always sleep at daybreak.
— Not a bad idea, another of the dervishes said with a smile.

Three of the dervishes turned to the one who had called out to the Lord. 'Why don't you start?' they said.

Shaikh, I shall tell you the first dervish's story tomorrow evening. Go to bed now. You have to go out with Kimia tomorrow morning.

FIVE

It's our second evening, Shaikh. Let us hear the first dervish tell his story.

The dervish looked at the sky for some time and then said, 'Then allow me to tell you the story.'

— Please begin, the other three dervishes said in unison.

— You've heard of Khvajah Ahmad, the merchant from Yemen, haven't you?

— Zaroor.

— He is my father. His business interests were spread out across the world. My only sister moved to a different city after her marriage. My father ensured an education for me, but destiny dealt a hidden blow.

— What happened? One of the dervishes asked.

— My parents died when I was fourteen. I became an orphan. But who else could manage my father's business besides me? I had to shoulder the entire responsibility at that age. You cannot even imagine how much wealth Khvajah Ahmad had left behind. I started life in my own way. I was just fourteen, I had seen nothing of the world.

I believed everything that people told me. Soon I was surrounded by people who constantly extolled my abilities and led me into a life of pleasure. They taught me to enjoy wine and the company of women. And I was swept away in this sea of sensual happiness. As you know, the Devil comes to us in the guise of humans. Once you have been captivated by the flesh of a woman, your life goes out of control. I began to squander my father's accumulated wealth on wine, women and gambling.

— Which means you became bankrupt eventually, didn't you? Another of the dervishes asked with a smile.

— This was the Lord's way of teaching me a lesson. Those who had enjoyed themselves on my money were the first to leave. They didn't even spare a glance for me anymore. No money, no friends, not even two meals a day—this was my condition as I wandered about on the roads. One day, a friend who was passing didn't even acknowledge me when I called out to him. I was close to starving to death. That was when I decided to go to my sister. But I was ashamed of the fact that I had not enquired after her even once after the death of my father.

— That's what happens, Shaikh, we don't remember the ones closest to us when we're happy, one of the other dervishes said.

— Yes, every hour of pleasure is actually the hour of the devil, sighed another of the dervishes.

— I arrived at my sister's house. She broke down in tears and put her arms around me when she saw that I was a pauper now. How did it happen, she kept asking me. My guilt didn't let me answer. My sister wiped away all my pain with her love and affection. The delicious food and rest at her house refreshed me. But fate didn't let me enjoy this very long.

— Why should it? One of the dervishes smiled. — If you make even a single mistake, the Lord will test you many times before he lets you finish life's journey.

— You're right, Shaikh.

The first dervish was sunk in thought for a long time.

— Finish your story, Shaikh.

— Yes. One day my sister told me . . .

— The Lord has given you a new life, Bhaijaan. I don't want to be parted from you anymore.

— I don't want to go away from you either. I have no wish to die in some barren land somewhere.

— But you must find yourself something to do.

— Do what?

— What will people say if you don't earn a living? They will say, first he frittered away his father's wealth, and now he's living off his brother-in-law. Our parents will be brought into dishonour, Bhaijaan. So you must be engaged in some kind of work.

— That's what I'd like too. You are my mother now, I'll do as you say.

— My sister kissed my forehead and left. She was back soon with several of her maids. They placed fifty sacks filled with gold coins in front of me. My sister said . . .

— A caravan of merchants will be leaving for Damascus in a day or two. I want you to go with them. You can use these coins to buy goods that you can sell at a profit in Damascus. But first we must find an honest merchant.

— Why?

— You must entrust all your goods to him so that he can sell them. The merchants will travel by sea, but you will go on horseback. You must make sure he accounts for every penny he has received for your goods.

— I followed my sister's instructions scrupulously. The merchants' ship sailed two days later. I left on horseback for Damascus with some food. It was not a long journey. It was night when I arrived, and the gates to the city were closed.

— How about some kumis, Shaikh? Yaqut al-Mustasimi asked me.

— The story . . .

— The story can continue over a drink. Did you know that those who drink kumis never harm anyone?

— I didn't know that.

— The ancients told us all this.

Travelling around Turkistan, truth be told, I fell in love with kumis. It's made by fermenting the milk of a mare. Mare's milk is far superior to cow's milk in some respects. I learnt all this only when I came to Turkistan. Mare's milk is lower on fat and higher on sugar, which makes fermentation very easy. But kumis cannot be made from any mare's milk. She must be allowed to roam in open fields, and she must have given birth to at least two foals before being milked. The milk can be collected two months after she gives birth, and she must be given clean surroundings in the open to live in. She must be fed regularly, given plenty of water to drink, and have a diet of plants rich in sugar.

Sipping his kumis, Yaqut al-Mustasimi resumed his story.

— Now hear the dervish tell the rest of the story, Shaikh.
— Very well.

The dervish continued his tale. — The sentries refused to open the gate despite all my requests. I dismounted from my horse, threw the reins on the ground, and sat down. Such deep silence! I simply couldn't sleep, I just kept pacing up and down, and the night deepened. Suddenly, something strange happened.

— What?
— An enormous chest was let down over the wall at the end of a rope. I thought it was a miracle. Had the Lord been kind and sent me a huge chest of jewels?
— The Lord is merciful, said one of the dervishes.
— Allahu Akbar. The other two dervishes joined the Zikr.
— It was a wooden chest. I opened it hastily, and my eyes nearly popped out.
— What sort of jewels did it hold, Shaikh?
— Just the one. I cannot explain how beautiful she was. But she was injured, and the blood on her garments had not dried yet. I couldn't turn my eyes away from her beauty. She was muttering some words. Lowering my face to hers, I heard her saying, 'So this is how you pay me back for being good to you, devil? Kill me then, kill me. Allah will

ensure justice.' Unknown to myself, I said, 'Which devil would want to kill such a beautiful woman? And yet she's talking about him.'

— And then?

— When the woman heard me speak she drew her veil aside to look at me. As you know, a single glance can turn the world upside down. Love is born. I almost fainted.

— No one faints, Shaikh, said one of the dervishes, laughing. — They only pretend to faint.

— Mashallah! So true! Another of the dervishes slapped his own thigh.

— I asked her, 'Who are you? Who has tortured you like this?' And she replied in a faint voice . . .

— The Lord is merciful. I cannot talk anymore. When I die please bury me in this chest, somewhere where no one can find me, where no one can speak ill of me. That is all I pray. The Lord shall take care of you.

Yaqut al-Mustasimi paused, taking slow sips of his kumis. An apprentice calligraphist was playing the flute in his workshop downstairs. Mustasimi nodded in time as he drank. Finally he said, 'How colourless the sunlight is, Shaikh. The walls have no colour either. Love ends. The light keeps changing. I need his compassion even more than I had imagined, Shaikh. I have often prayed to Allah, have mercy. How can I continue with my tale without his mercy?

— Finish the story, janab, dawn is near, I said.

— Then hear it the way the dervish told it. Who am I to speak on his behalf?

The dervish resumed his story. — I kept the chest under

my protection. Where could I have gone at that hour of the night? Finally morning came with the call of the rooster and the Muezzin's azaan. Completing the early-morning namaz, I entered the city on horseback with the chest. Had I been by myself I would have stayed at an inn. But there was a woman inside the chest. So I had to rent a house. The servant was excellent. When I told him all the details, he told me of a doctor who was well versed in surgery. Tracking down his house from the address, I arrived there. The aged doctor asked, running his hand through his beard . . .

— Alive or dead?

— Alive.

— Good, we might be able to do something then. Who is she?

— My wife.

— Everyone says that. The doctor, named Insha, smiled toothlessly. — Anyone who brings a woman to Damascus claims she is his wife. A regular affair. Which of your wives is she?

— The first and only one, janab.

— How strange! You're satisfied with just one?

— Yes. I'm in Damascus on business. I've brought my wife along because I love her so much.

— How long have you been married?

— Two years.

Insha the doctor burst into laughter. — Let five years pass. Then the bitter taste will creep in. Now tell me what happened . . .

— When night fell we stopped our journey to take shelter beneath a tree. At midnight we were attacked by dacoits. Not only did they take all we had, they also left my wife badly wounded. I entered the city this morning. I've been told no one can match you as a surgeon. My wife's life will be saved if you treat her.

Without another word the doctor accompanied me home. Examining the woman, he said, 'The wounds are very serious, but if Allah so wills it, she will recover in forty days.'

Soaking neem leaves in water, he washed her wounds with it, stitching some of them, applying ointment on others and bandaging them. Stroking her forehead, he said, 'I'll change the bandages every morning. Make sure your wife rests all day. Give her some strong chicken soup every day.'

— Are you sleepy, Shaikh? Yaqut al-Mustasimi asked me.

— No.

— Do you want to hear the entire story tonight?

— I do.

— You'll go with Kimia tomorrow morning to herd the sheep, won't you?

— I will.

— Then continue with your story, dervish.

— Very well. I had earned handsomely from the sale of the goods I had brought to Damascus. But all of it was spent on the woman's treatment. Insha the doctor would visit every day. Gradually the beautiful woman regained her health. I felt indescribably happy. One day she told me . . .

— Mian.
— Yes?
— A question.
— Yes?
— If you want me to be happy, you'll do whatever I ask you to do, won't you?
— Of course.
— You must never ask why.
— Why not?
— Because you'll have to repent if you do.
— There's nothing worse than remorse in life.
— Then don't ask me any questions.

One of the dervishes said, 'Clearly you were in a difficult situation.'

— Yes, but I never asked her any questions. Meanwhile, I was running out of money. I didn't know anyone in Damascus. My anxiety grew. It was probably because she understood this that she said one day . . .

— I will never forget all that you've done for me.
— I love you.

Smiling, she said, 'Forget about love. People do things for one another. These are the Lord's instructions. What else are you a Muslim for? Now listen to me . . .

— Tell me.
— I cannot pay you back all the money you have spent on me.
— Have I ever asked you to?
— No, but I can make out you're worried. What you can do is . . .

Smiling, I said, 'Throw you out?'

— You cannot do that. Nor shall I let that happen. But there's something you can do . . .

— What is that?

— Get me a sheet of paper, a pen and some ink.

— Why?

— The condition was that you wouldn't ask questions.

— I brought her paper, a pen and an ink pot. Writing a note, she told me, 'There's a large palace on the road leading to the fort. Sidi Bahar lives there. This letter must reach his hands.'

Suddenly Yaqut al-Mustasimi rose to his feet.

— Aren't you going to finish the story? I asked.

— It's very late, Shaikh. Kimia cannot sleep till I get back. A foundling, you see. She has no one of her own. And moreover, this qissa is very long. It has tired me out.

— Then you'd better go to bed.

— Can I ask you something, Shaikh?

— Of course.

— Do you like Kimia?

— Very much, I said effusively.

— In what way do you like her? Like a lover or like a sister?

I was silent. Placing his hand on my shoulder, Yaqut al-Mustasimi said, 'Will you take her with you?'

— Where?

— On your journey. I shan't live much longer. Who will take care of her, Shaikh?

SIX

We are welcoming our third evening, Shaikh Ibn Battuta. The first dervish reached Sidi Bahar's palace to deliver the beautiful woman's letter. Listen to his story while you sip your kumis.

— Carry on, janab.

The dervish continued. — A young black man greeted me, disappearing inside the palace with the letter. He came back a little later, followed by eleven slaves balancing muslin-covered pots on their heads. He directed them to accompany me home and deliver the vessels. The eleven pots were filled to the brim with gold coins. The woman only said, 'You needn't worry about expenses anymore.' But this money was now a cause for concern . . .

— Naturally, said one of the dervishes.

— It's very suspicious for a stranger to give you so much money simply on the strength of a letter, without asking any questions. Didn't you ask her what was going on?

— Questions were prohibited, as you know. But I was not at peace. One day she told me, 'I don't like seeing you in these clothes. Go to the market and buy some stylish clothes at Yusuf's shop.'

— Did you go?

— Yes, I couldn't disobey her instructions. The sight of Yusuf in his saffron clothes warmed my heart. His conversation attracted me like a magnet. He asked me who I was and where I had come from. I was forced to lie. Suddenly he held my arm, saying . . .

— I've never liked anyone as much as you, janab.

— Khuda meherban!

— Stay with me tonight. Some of my friends are coming too.

— So you stayed the night? One of the dervishes asked.

— No . . . no. How could I stay out all night without seeking the beautiful woman's permission? I told her everything when I went back home. She said, 'Since he's invited you, you must go. Don't worry about me. The Lord will look after me.'

— I do not wish to leave you here alone. But now you're saying . . . Yet my heart tells me . . .

— Tells you what? She laughed, jiggling her knees.

— I couldn't protest any more.

— Alas! One of the dervishes smacked himself on the forehead. — So you abandoned a beautiful woman for the company of a shopkeeper!

— It was her command.

— Women issue many commands, must each and every one be followed? Anyway, go on.

— I was overwhelmed by Yusuf's hospitality. Such a huge

garden, a waterfall, flowering plants. Saqis distributing wine in crystal goblets. Four beautiful young men began to sing. One is seldom fortunate enough to spend the night with such young men these days. The lustre of their chests and buttocks beats many beautiful women.

— Did you spend the night with any of them?
— No.
— Why not?
— My beautiful woman was alone at home . . . I kept recalling her face. And to tell the truth, I was never attracted to beautiful young men.

Yaqut al-Mustasimi was becoming drowsy. Pouring kumis into his glass, I said, 'Pardon my insolence, but may I ask a question?'

— Of course.
— While travelling to Anatolia I heard many people say that Maulana was a homosexual. What is your opinion?

Mustasimi began to tremble. Then he shouted, 'Is this all you want to know about Maulana?'

— No.
— Then why do you ask? Is it because he spent forty days in a room with Shams Tabrizi? Is it because Hussamuddin Chalabi wrote down his Masnavi from Maulana's oral version? Then you should know, Shaikh, that Maulana made love with his second wife Kira Khatun eighty times during a single night. Never mind all that, what is your view on homosexuality, Shaikh?

— Homosexuality is profane, janab.
— Why?

— It is not desired by nature.

— Who says this? Who are they who say this? Were you the one who decided the kind of sexual desire you were born with, Shaikh? Isn't it nature who gave birth to you that way? There are many people who are equally attracted to women and men. Their mother is nature. Who are they? What will you call them? Will you exclude them from society?

— But this form of sexual desire is not accepted by society.

— If you think about acceptance or rejection by society, you won't be able to read my munaqib about Maulana, Shaikh. Do you want to hear the rest of the story?

— Yes, tell me.

— Then let us listen to what the first dervish is saying . . .

— As we were in raptures over the music and the wine, Yusuf suddenly said, 'I have nothing to hide from you, my friend. Let me send for my beloved then. My life is colourless without her.'

— No celebration is possible without your mashuqa, my friend. Please ask her to join us, I said.

— I know what you saw, said one of the dervishes.

— You do?

— A woman looking like a black witch came out from behind the curtain, isn't that right?

— Yes. How did you know?

— The Lord told me. Go on.

— How could a handsome man like Yusuf have such an ugly lover? The question ate away at me. After three days and nights immersed in the flow of music and wine, I returned home guiltily. When I asked the beautiful woman to forgive me, she said, 'You were right. You cannot return till the host permits you to. Now you have one more task.'

— What's that?

— Aren't you going to invite your friend? You have to do twice as much as he did for you. Don't worry about the expenses, the Lord will make the arrangements.

— Although Yusuf refused at first, he agreed eventually. But on my way back I wondered what I had with which to keep him happy. He would visit that evening, I had hardly any means to entertain him.

— But all the arrangements had been made, hadn't they? One of the dervishes asked with a smile.

— Yes, I was astonished as I approached my house. The road had been washed, there wasn't a trace of filth anywhere. When I entered I discovered patterned carpets, cushions in different colours, vases filled with flowers, syringes to sprinkle rosewater, vials of expensive perfume, bowls of paan, camphor flames in golden lamps. A regal sight. The fragrance of cooking was everywhere.

— And then? One of the dervishes asked.

— Yusuf arrived on time. Looking for the beautiful woman in order to introduce them to each other, I found her in the kitchen. She was dressed plainly, a scarf covering her head. She was giving instructions on how and when the food was to be served. When I saw her I felt that a woman whose beauty comes from the Lord needs no other embellishment. She is always a full moon. Charmed by the ease with which she got the cooks to do her bidding, I showered effusive praise on her.

— And you must have heard abuse in return. Women are very strange, Shaikh. They mope if you don't say anything, but if you praise them . . .

— Do you know what she told me? 'I haven't done anything to deserve such praise. You shouldn't have left your guest alone, janab. What must he be thinking? You must invite his beloved too. Or else he will be lonely.' Yusuf looked very eager when I suggested sending for his mashuqa. I sent a eunuch with a palanquin to fetch her.

One of the dervishes burst into laughter.

— Why do you laugh? The first dervish asked.

— I've been troubled by a question for some time. Do any of you know the answer?

— What is it?

— Does becoming a eunuch kill desire?

All four dervishes lowered their heads. The questioner continued, 'Do you know the source of desire?'

— The body, said one of the dervishes.

— And where does the body come from? From Khuda's pen, right?

— Yes, he writes us.

— Aren't the memories stored in that pen passed on to our bodies? Can anyone forget them even as a eunuch? Even if they've lost the ability they can still feel the pleasure, can't they?

— Yes.

— Then what do we conclude?

— What?

— The eunuch is the observer who has not been told by Allah to apply his abilities. In our old age we men become eunuchs too, but does that mean we don't enjoy the beauty of women? I have often been aroused by the sight of a pair of grapes in contact with muslin.

— Two grapes at the tip of two peaches, exclaimed one of the other dervishes.

— Marhabba! Now finish your story, Shaikh.

— Three days and three nights of pleasure passed in a flash. Not once did I drink with Yusuf and his lover, lest the beautiful woman in my house be angry. On the fourth day Yusuf sought to take my leave, requesting me to drink with him. I could not turn down a guest's last request. That night we fell asleep drinking.

Yaqut al-Mustasimi sat in silence for a long time. Drowsily he said, 'I'm sleepy too, Shaikh.'

— Will the story remain unfinished tonight too?

— I can't write my munaqib quickly.

— Why not?

— Like a frightened deer Maulana keeps running away from me.

— But I cannot stay here much longer.

— I know. You have to see the entire world. I am old. Let me rest tonight. I will work harder on the munaqib from tomorrow, and tell you the dervish's story in the evening too.

— But janab, it will take a long time to copy your munaqib after you've finished it.

— I'll give you the original. Al-Mustasimi smiled.
— What are you saying?
— The original will remain in the book in my heart. Then I will go to my grave. All the words will mingle with the earth. The story of Maulana's life will also be buried in the soil. Let me go now. You'd better sleep too, Shaikh. You have to go out with Kimia in the morning, don't you?

SEVEN

'Welcome to the fourth evening,' Al-Mustasimi smiled at me.

After a short silence the first dervish resumed his story.

— That night we all went to sleep under the influence of the wine. When I awoke the next morning I found the house empty. It seemed to have been turned into Karbala. I couldn't even find the beautiful woman anywhere. Something lay wrapped in a blanket in one corner of the room we had fallen asleep in. When I unwrapped it what I saw terrified me.

— What did you see? one of the dervishes asked.

— The headless bodies of my guest Yusuf and his lover.

— Ya Allah! All three dervishes shrieked.

— I was turned into stone. Who had done this? And where was the beautiful woman? Suddenly spotting the eunuch who had fetched Yusuf's lover, I ran up to him to ask, 'What's all this? Who has done this?'

Smiling, the eunuch said, 'It's no use asking, huzoor.'

— Where's your mistress?

— An intelligent man like you drank yourself into a stupor without taking her permission. And with whom? With someone whom you met only a few days ago.

— Don't talk that way. He was my guest.

— A guest after just a few days of acquaintance?

I stammered, 'I can see I made a mistake. But where is your mistress? I have to apologize to her.'

— What happened to the corpses? a dervish asked.

— The eunuch buried them.

— Did you locate the beautiful woman?

— Yes, the eunuch gave me her address. After a long search I found her house in the evening.

— Did you meet her?

— No. I was afraid to enter. I sat outside all night. At dawn a window opened. I caught a glimpse of her. My heart leapt with joy, but the window closed at once. A little later, a eunuch came up to me and said, 'There's a mosque ahead. Go there and wait. You'll get whatever you need.'

Sipping his kumis, Al-Mustasimi chuckled.

— Why do you laugh? I asked.

— Can you tell me whether the merchant's son from Yemen and the beautiful woman were married later or not?

Scratching my head, I said, 'Yes . . . yes, they were, janab.'

— How did you know?

— They wouldn't have met otherwise.

— Yes! Indeed! Al-Mustasimi clapped. — You have understood the intricacies of this tale. But some more incidents took place before the wedding. The beautiful woman was in fact the daughter of the Sultan of Damascus. Her life had also passed through many ups and downs.

— What happened before they were married?

— The merchant's son met the beautiful woman, who turned him away. When he had been wandering for forty days without food and was at the doorstep of death, that same eunuch found him on the streets and took him to the beautiful woman. The eunuch persuaded the Sultan's daughter to arrange for the merchant's son to be treated. When he recovered, he got married to the Sultan's daughter. Now let us listen to the rest of the story from the dervish.

The first dervish said heavily, 'It was true that my heart was filled with joy when my beloved became mine, but several questions were beginning to haunt me.'

— What questions?

— Who was the young black man who gave me all those pots of gold coins? How was that elaborate feast organized? Why were my guests murdered? Who killed them? Why did someone who had thrown me out accept me later? These questions troubled me so much that I could not be comfortable with my wife. Eight days and eight nights passed after the wedding, but I could not share a bed with her. Finally she asked me . . .

— What's the matter with you? You were desperate to marry me, and now you don't want to come anywhere near me. What's happened to you?

— Bowing my head, I said, 'People want justice, Bibijaan.'

— Haven't you got justice? You've got what you wanted.

— Of course. I had wanted you with all my heart and by the grace of god I've got you too. But . . .

— What else do you want?

— I cannot make sense of all that has happened. It's all a mystery to me. Explain everything to me, Bibijaan, so that I can be comfortable again.

My wife exploded in anger. — You have probably forgotten your promise. I had said you mustn't ask any questions.

— You are my wife now. You shouldn't keep any secrets from me.

Suddenly she quietened down. After a short silence, she said, 'That's true. But we may be in danger if you know everything.'

— Think of the dangers we have overcome, Bibijaan, I told her, taking her hands. — Trust me and tell me. No one else will come to know.

My wife smiled sarcastically. — It is foolish to want to know everything. I'm certain it will lead us into danger. But since you are my husband, I cannot keep anything from you.

Now the Sultan of Damascus's daughter began her story. 'I am the Sultan's only child. My parents loved me very much. Those were such wonderful times, like pages from a book written in golden ink. As a child I used to like beautiful girls, spending all my time in their company. All the maids were beautiful too. But I went through a strange transformation one day. My heart was bereft, as though I had lost something. I no longer liked the company of women, nor did I enjoy talking to anyone. This favourite eunuch of mine could read my mind, and I never hid anything from him. He understood my suffering. One day he told me, beti huzrain, I have a suggestion.

— Tell me.
— Have a little wine.
— What are you saying! I was startled.
— Try it. You'll feel lighter, and you'll regain your happiness.
— Are you sure?
— Have I ever failed to be of service to you, beti huzrain?
— All right, bring me some wine, then.

The eunuch appeared a little later with a young boy, who placed an intricately patterned goblet before me. As I drank, I realized that the eunuch was right. Giving the boy some money, I told him, 'Bring me some wine at this hour every day.'

Gradually my life returned to me. I used to play with the boy, chat with him. He told me amusing stories. I was more and more attracted to him. Every day I used to give him an expensive gift or some money. But he was always shabbily dressed. One day I said, 'I give you money every day, but still you dress in rags. Do you spend all the money?'

He stood in silence for a long time. I saw his eyes filling with tears. A chilly wind seemed to blow over my heart. Someone seemed to pronounce a single word in my head, mashuqa, my beloved. I was close to tears too. 'What's the matter?' I asked him.

Weeping, he said, 'My master takes away all the money

you give me. He doesn't give me any of it. I can't afford new clothes.'

Beloved. My beloved. How could I allow him to be someone's slave? I told the eunuch, buy him new clothes, take him under your wing, he must become worthy of me. The eunuch could not disobey me. The boy grew more and more handsome and I couldn't take my eyes off him. Every time I saw him I wanted to hold him in my arms.

After a short silence Al-Mustasimi said, 'Nobody can tell where love will transport them. Not even the Lord. Maulana had written, my soul is an oven, an oven that's alight wants nothing but love. If you do not wish to be burnt in its flames, my friend, you still have a lot left to learn.

— How much longer will this story go on, janab? I asked.

— Are you becoming impatient?

— Not at all.

— Listen, Shaikh, this story is rich with creepers and leaves and flowers. You could say it's a garden. Presenting a garden like this should take a thousand nights. But we won't live that long. That's why I'm forced to condense the whole story. There are so many things I haven't told you. Have I described the beauty of the Sultan's daughter? Have I given you details about her house? Didn't I tell you it would take a thousand nights? I am saddened to have to present a story without all this. A qissa is not just a succession of events, it includes embellishments, it involves patterns. But you don't have the time, and neither do I. You have to leave, and I have to finish my munaqib on Maulana's life and hand it over to you. So we will not have the opportunity to listen to the stories told by the other three dervishes, or to the tale of Sultan Azad Bakht. Come, let's resume our qissa. Do you want to hear it in my words or in the Sultan's daughter's?

— Let her tell the story.

The Sultan's daughter continued, 'I used to give him whatever he wanted. I would become restless when he wasn't near me. Suddenly I discovered he had turned into a young man, and I, a young woman. He was barred from entering the ladies' quarters. But how was I to live without him? Oh my Lord, show me a way to have my beloved by my side. Summoning the eunuch, I told him to ensure that my young man lacked for nothing. Give him one thousand gold coins and ask him to open a jewellery shop in the market. He should buy a house close to mine. The servants and maids should take care of his needs.'

— Such women exist only in stories, janab, I said with a smile.

Al-Mustasimi smiled too. — These things don't happen in real life. If I could have found a Sultan's daughter such as she, I would have been her slave. You would also have lost your passion for travelling around the world, Shaikh. Never mind, let us listen to the Sultan's daughter tell us what happened after this.

— The young man's business prospered. His was the only shop which stocked the clothes and ornaments needed by sultans and navabs and kings and ministers. I was delighted at the news. But I could no longer bear the burden of not being able to see him. On the eunuch's advice, it was decided to dig a tunnel connecting his house to mine. The eunuch was resourceful, and the tunnel was ready in a few days. He would bring my young man to see me every evening. He would stay with me all night, leaving when the morning azaan was heard. A long time passed this way. I bought him a huge mansion with a garden to fulfil his wishes. He got a female slave along with the mansion. One day, I went into the tunnel with a maid to take a look at his house. The garden was so beautiful that it could be compared only to the gardens of paradise. I strolled around the garden all day. When he came home from the market in the evening and saw me, he held me in his arms at once. There was a full moon in the sky. He took me to the balcony. I put my arms around him and buried my face in his chest. Suddenly a hag arrived with a goblet of wine. I had never seen such an ugly woman before.

— Who is she?
— The slave who came with the mansion. I was furious. How could such an ugly woman be my wine-bearer? This was akin to the insolence of keeping a nightingale and a crow in the same cage. But what could I have done anyway? I had no choice but to drink with them. The shameless hussy got drunk and flirted outrageously with him. My beloved also lost all his inhibitions with the brazen woman. But still I said nothing, because I loved him so much. I assumed he had drunk too much. As soon as I rose to leave, he threw himself at my feet,

begging my pardon repeatedly. When I saw the tears in his eyes I had to stay back. He forced two more goblets of wine on me. I was nearly unconscious. That was when the traitor attacked me with his sword, gouging out my flesh. I gave him a single glance, saying, 'You have indeed given me what I deserve.' I didn't remember anything more. Assuming I was dead, he packed me into a chest and slung me over the city walls.

Al-Mustasimi said, 'Can you tell me the reason for the Sultan's daughter's plight, Shaikh?'

— Bad judgement about people.

— No. Her eyes. Our eyes are our enemy. We fall in love at first sight with things that destroy us later. Never trust what you see with your eyes, Shaikh. Maulana said, you must turn into a ruby on the road to love. A ruby that looks at the sun. Another world of red. Let's return to the story.

Then the Sultan's daughter told her husband, the merchant's son, 'By the Lord's grace you were near the wall that night, which is how my life was returned to me. Believe me, I had no wish to live. But death is not in one's own hands. Suicide is not Allah's way. And your attention and tenderness made me learn to love life afresh. I realized that kindness is much greater than love. Infatuation is often a part of love, but it has no role to play in kindness. When I saw you had run out of money after spending it all on me, I sent you to Sidi Bahar. He maintained the accounts of my wealth. In the letter I informed him that I was safe, and requested him to pass the news on to my mother. The Yusuf whose shop I sent you to was my beloved. I had realized that an arrogant wretch like him would want to befriend you and invite you home. Do I have to explain what happened afterwards? It was I who ordered Yusuf and his ugly female slave to be beheaded.'

— So you took revenge, said the merchant's son.

— Yes.

— Are you happy?

The Sultan's daughter was silent. Her eyes filled with tears. 'No,' she said in a trembling voice. 'Now I wonder why I did all this.'

— You had loved Yusuf once, didn't you? He went astray, but you shouldn't have killed him for that reason, Bibijaan. And the slave did you no harm. If you allow me, may I say something?

— Yes.

— You never loved Yusuf. You wanted to possess him. So you gave him gifts every day to please him. Yusuf didn't love you either, he only wanted your wealth.

— I want to go away from this city.

— So we shall, Bibijaan. I don't know whether I love you, but it is the husband's duty to stay by his wife through all her joys and sorrows. I will perform my duty all my life.

Al-Mustasimi stood up. — Come with me, Shaikh.

We went up to the roof. Pointing to the darkness in front of us, Al-Mustasimi said, 'There, look.'

— Look at what?

— Can't you see?

— No.

— Open your inner eyes, Shaikh. You can see the

merchant's son and the Sultan's daughter leaving Damascus on a pair of spirited horses. After journeying a long way they will rest by a lake, they'll have to eat too. Then they will start riding again. You may not recognize the Sultan's daughter, for she is dressed like a man now. Now listen to their conversation . . .

— For you I have left my parents, my wealth, my homeland. You won't ever betray me, will you?

— All men are not the same, Bibijaan. Remember that I'm the slave whom you cannot buy with money. I'll use my skin to make shoes for you if need be. Never ask this question again.

— Shaikh . . . Al-Mustasimi called out to me.

— Yes, janab?

— This is what Maulana calls ishq. Make me your servant. There they are, day after day, night after night, riding away on their horses. Exhausted, they will finally dismount in a forest. They will hunt birds, roast them on a fire and eat them, and resume their journey. One day they will stop on the bank of a wide river, its water stretching as far as the eye can see. Allah, how will we cross this unending water? It's impossible without a boat. Asking his wife to wait, the merchant's son will set off in search of a boat. But there won't be a boat or boatman to be found anywhere.

— And then?

— When the merchant's son returns, he will not find the Sultan's daughter, Shaikh. He searched everywhere, but he could not locate her. The merchant's son returned to Damascus. He was practically a naked fakir by then, searching for his wife on the roads of Damascus.

— Where did the Sultan's daughter vanish?

Al-Mustasimi smiled, his eyes enigmatic. — Who can tell? Only the story knows where she vanished. Our first dervish will speak now. Let him tell us what happened.

The first dervish said, 'My life turned barren without her. One day I climbed a mountain with the intention of plunging into a ravine. As I was about to leap, someone held me back by my arm. Turning round, I saw a figure in a green robe sitting on a horse, his face covered. He said . . .

— Why do you want to take this road to death, my friend? As long as there is life, there is hope.

— Who are you?

— Listen to me. In a few days you will meet three dervishes in Constantinople. Like you, they too are wounded, people who have been dealt many blows by life. Azad Bakht, the Sultan of Turkistan, also lives with the burden of sorrows. Once you have met him, all of you will find your wishes coming true. Didn't you want to know who I am? I am Murtaza Ali. My job is to relieve the sorrows of suffering people.

— And then? one of the dervishes asked.

— Murtaza Ali melted into the air. I set off. And today, all four of us have met here in Constantinople by the grace of Shaikh Ali.

— Allahu Akbar! One of the dervishes called out a Zikr. The other three joined him.

Al-Mustasimi's stories and the copying of his munaqib on Maulana were nearing completion. That night Al-Mustasimi told me, 'A copy has been made of the book, Shaikh. You can leave tomorrow. It isn't right to stay too long in the same place.'

— Pray to the Lord that I may see the entire world.

— I am sure you will.

Late at night there was a knock on my door. Kimia was standing outside.

— Go well, Muhammad.

— Aren't you coming with me?

— You must come with me first. Kimia took my hand.

I entered the sheep pen downstairs with her. They were all asleep. The pen was heavy with the sounds of their breathing. Running her hand gently across the body of a lamb, Kimia said, 'Who'll take them grazing?'

— Aren't you coming with me, Kimia? My mouth spoke, as though I were an actor.

— They won't survive if I go away, Muhammad.

Kimia began to caress the sleeping sheep. Who was caressing the lambs? Was it Kimia or was it Mary?

The next morning I joined a caravan of travellers to set off again.

I no longer had the time to listen to the stories of the other three dervishes and the tale of Sultan Azad Bakht.

EIGHT

My learned readers, I know many of you are losing your patience. But this preamble was necessary. In this book that I am about to read to you, the lives and times depicted are so distant from ours, its fragrance so unlike the smells we are used to, that it will be like wandering about in a perfumery where spring has expressed itself in its fullness, which is why we had to negotiate the labyrinth of other stories before taking our place in this vernal season. One more thing. When I opened the book at its first page to start reading, someone seemed to emerge from inside me to ask, 'Shaikh, don't you know what Maulana used to tell Hussam?'

— What?

— As he dictated the poems in his Masnavi, Maulana would often pause to ask, 'Who is playing this melody, Hussam?'

— Who?

After a pause Maulana would say, 'Let the maestro

complete the poem himself, Hussam.' Shaikh, let him talk through this book of yours. Don't you know why language and music are born?

— Because we are empty, devoid of anything?

— We are banished from where we came. We speak, write—all of it is driven by our need to return home.

My learned readers, remember that the kitab I am about to read from is at once written and not written by me. What does it matter, anyway? As you know, in Persian poetry it was customary for the poets to mention their takhallus, their pen name, at the very end. So let silence swallow this book. We want to hear its memory of the home it has left behind, and the tale of its return to that home from silence.

The person whom I have been referring to as Maulana all this time was Jalaluddin Muhammad Balkhi, who will gradually be transformed into Jalaluddin Muhammad Rumi. His journey was from a life in exile to his home. Under Allah's instructions and by Maulana's wish, I shall address him as Maulana or Rumi from now on. Rumi would start every volume of his Masnavi in verse with a prayer in prose. It was in such a prayer that he included a poem by the Andalusian poet Adi al-Riga.

> I slept in the arms of a cold wind
> A grey dove sang out from a thicket
> When I heard her sobs of longing
> I was reminded of my old passion
> I have been away so long from my soul

Such prolonged sleep, but I awoke too
In a sea of tears at the dove's weeping
Sing praises to the oppressed who rise early

Look, a caravan has set out from the city of Balkh in Khorasan. It was here that Jalaluddin Muhammad was born in Hijri 604, or 1207 AD. Balkh was known as the dome of Islam at the time of Rumi's birth. Centre of the high tide of commerce and education, steeped in Islam, and home to well-known ascetics. This was where the two Sufi saints Ibrahim ibn Adham and Shaqiq al-Balkhi had once lived. Shaikh Najmuddin Kubra, founder of the Kubrawiyya order, was alive in Rumi's childhood. When I went to the town of Balkh, I saw nothing but ruins. It felt as though the world had lost a dream. The Mongols wiped out many memories and dream towns this way. Had Maulana heard my lament he would surely have said, 'Nature wipes everything out, as it must. Who are you and I to worry about this?'

In the caravan that is wending its way forward are Bahauddin Walad, his wife Momina Khatun, their sons Alauddin Muhammad and Jalaluddin Muhammad, along with some of Bahauddin's students. There aren't too many household effects, but Bahauddin's collection of books is loaded on the backs of several camels: the Quran, different manuscripts on the Hadith, a number of books on religion and Islamic law. Bahauddin was known as the Sultan-ul Ulema, King of Religious Scholars. He was both an ulema and a Sufi saint. Several generations of this family of scholars had lived in Balkh. There are various views on why Bahauddin decided to leave home. One reason was the apprehension of a Mongol invasion. But what I heard in Balkh was that unlike Bahauddin, his teacher Najmuddin Kubra did not abandon the city out of fear of the Mongols—he fought them with his disciples till his last breath.

All this is real, my learned readers, but does it not seem like a fable now? Then I might as well tell you a story. The only treasures I have gathered on all my travels around the world are these qissas. Maulana Rumi told this story in his Masnavi. He will speak to us now:

Listen then, Hussam, my friend, my dearest, greater than my soul, Hussam, let me tell you about the musk deer. An innocent and feeble deer. Is it I, Hussam? Lean, pale, with bushy eyebrows and reddish brown eyes, like a lonely almond. A deer like this is bound to be a victim of fate. A hunter caught him and put him in a cattle shed. The shed was filled with bulls and asses. Reeling, the musk deer eventually fell unconscious. He had tried so many times to escape, but all the doors were locked. When all the doors are locked, you cannot get out—have you ever found yourself being dragged down into such filth and slime, Hussam? In the evening the hunter brought hay to feed the imprisoned animals. But hay was for bulls and asses. The poor musk deer had never eaten it. He passed days without any food. You know how a fish feels when it is taken out of water. The bulls and the asses thought the deer was extremely arrogant. An ass mocked him, 'Why is an emperor like you languishing in this cattle shed?'

The musk deer told the ass, 'No, it isn't arrogance. Hay is what you eat. I roam about in the fields, fresh grass and water are my food and drink. I may be far from home, my friend, but still I'm a musk deer. I may be a pauper, but my soul hasn't been impoverished.'

Laughing, the ass said, 'People say these meaningless things when they're homesick. You have to prove yourself, this timidity is of no use.'

— Look at my musk. It wasn't created by eating hay.

I know the bulls and the asses paid no heed to the musk deer, Hussam. Most people are like that. They make no attempt to look or listen or understand beyond their limitations. Let me tell you another story then.

— Should I write it down, Maulana?

— That's up to you. I'm not here to leave anything behind. I am only a spring day, I am merely a pea being boiled in a kettle. Listen, then. Travelling through the desert, a parched pilgrim saw a small tent. When he asked for water a woman did give him some, but it was as hot as fire, as saline as the sea. But what can come in the way of thirst? The water went down his throat, burning everything in its path. The pilgrim told the woman, 'You gave me water, I want to give you something in return. There are cities like Basra and Baghdad not far from here. They're full of delicious food, cold water, tasty sherbets. Why are you here in the desert?' A little later her husband brought some desert rats he had hunted. The rat meat was cooked. The pilgrim ate reluctantly. As he lay outside the tent, he heard the woman asking her husband whether they could leave the desert. Do you know what the husband said? 'Don't believe these people. They're jealous, they can't bear to see other people being happy.' What do you make of it, Hussam?

— They think of love as envy, Maulana.

— Love is like the water trickling through a crack in the rock, Hussam. How many people can see it?

The caravan rolled on. Rumi was nine. The first stop was at Nishapur. This was the home of Fariduddin Attar. His poetry was as fragrant as his perfumery. People far and wide know of his shop in this north-eastern town of Iran. Fariduddin was a doctor, a perfume-seller and a Sufi saint all at the same time. Egypt, Damascus, Mecca, Turkistan, India—he had travelled through numerous lands to understand the condition of people and the world.

Attar would visit Bahauddin's camp every evening. The Sultan-ul Ulema would be explaining Sharia law to his pupils at the time. Attar would draw the nine-year-old boy to himself, looking into his eyes. They were like hazelnuts, reddish brown. It seemed to Attar that they led to a winding road running beyond this world into another one.

Attar decided that his *Asrarnama*, which was a book of secrets, could be gifted to nobody but this boy. His writing would be fulfilled the day the boy grew up and read it.

Fariduddin Attar was right. Many years later, when Maulana dictated the verses of his Masnavi to Hussam, he included several of Attar's stories in his epic.

One day Attar clasped the boy to his breast. He felt that finally his long thirst had been quenched, he felt like a cloud in an autumn sky. 'Do you want to hear a story, Jalal?' he whispered.

— Yes, please. Who is it about?

— It's about birds.

— Which birds?

— Innumerable birds, they're out in search of their Sultan.

— Who's their Sultan?

— Simurgh.

— Who's Simurgh?

Every evening Attar told the boy of the journey of the birds. All these were the stories from his book. Led by their teacher, the hoopoe, a flock of innumerable birds are flying in search of their king. Snared by temptations and illusions along the way, many of them are unable to make the ascent.

— And then? asked Jalal, his reddish brown eyes glittering like jewels.

The sky was studded with stars. Attar took Jalal in his arms. Planting kisses on his forehead, cheeks and neck, he said, 'The birds flew for many, many years behind their teacher, the hoopoe, crossing not one or two but seven valleys. Many birds died on the way, many lost their ability to fly. Eventually just thirty birds reached Simurgh's palace on Qaf Mountain. The guards refused them entry. The birds waited for their emperor to send for them.'

— How long did they wait?

Attar smiled. 'You think I know? Only Allah does.'
— The birds didn't stay awake then?
— Who told you that?
— I've seen.
— What have you seen, Jalal?
— Birds stay awake.
— Now let me tell you about the miracle that followed. Eventually Emperor Simurgh's personal attendant appeared to escort them to his court. How strange! Wherever the birds looked, they could only see themselves, thirty birds staring at one another in wonder. Where was Simurgh, then?
— Where was he?
— Jalal, the word Simurgh means thirty birds. They were now face to face with their souls.

Bahauddin's caravan left Nishapur the next day. Bidding farewell to the Sultan-ul Ulema, Attar stood looking for a long time at the road along which they had departed. Bahauddin was walking, followed by the nine-year-old boy. Attar murmured, 'There goes the sea, and behind it the ocean. What a wondrous sight you have shown me today, Lord.'

They journeyed from Nishapur to Baghdad. All of you know of Baghdad, the centre of the Caliphate. A glittering metropolis! A crowd gathered around Bahauddin's caravan on the edge of the city. Who were these people? Where were they from? One of them stepped up to ask Bahauddin, 'Pardon me, where are you coming from?'

Bahauddin looked at him for a while before bursting into laughter. The crowd retreated a few steps.

— Why do you want to know? Bahauddin asked.

Fawning, the man said, 'You're guests of the city, so . . .'

— Hmm . . . Bahauddin ran his fingers through his beard. Then, looking up at the sky, he said, 'We have come from the Lord, my friend, and we'll go back to him too.'

Bahauddin's response spread throughout the city. Who was this man who belonged nowhere? Can you imagine, he said he's come from the Lord and he'll go back to him too. The whispers began. You couldn't look him in the eye as you talked to him. Your heart shrank when you stood in front of him.

We have come from the Lord, my friend, and we'll go back to him too. Hurtling through the air, the answer reached Shahabuddin Suhrawardi. The Sufi saint was startled. 'Where is he?' he shouted.

A pupil of his kneeled near his feet. 'He's in a tent outside the city.'

— Let's go at once. Inform the Caliph.

— Do you know him, Shaikh?

— Not know him? No one but Bahauddin Walad can say such a thing.

— Who is he?

— He's from Balkh. We must welcome him. Let me tell you a story from Shaikh Bahauddin's life. One day, he was rapt in thought, while the hour of the midday namaz was fast approaching. Bahauddin remained sitting, his eyes shut. His pupils kept telling him, 'It's time for the namaz, Shaikh.' Bahauddin remained as he was, without answering. Facing the qibla, the direction of the Kaaba, the pupils began to read the namaz, while Maulana Bahauddin remained sitting behind them. Only two of the pupils stayed back with their Shaikh instead of joining the others for the namaz. As they said their namaz, the students heard the voice of Allah. Do you know what the Lord said? 'The two who remained with the Shaikh are the only ones facing the qibla. Do you understand? The gap between you and me has been obliterated within Shaikh Bahauddin. What does the Hadith say? Die before you die. That is when the light goes on inside a person. If you turn your eyes away from that beam and face a wall of stone, your eyes are not turned towards the real qibla. Your Shaikh is your qibla. He who does not defer to his Shaikh will not be able to offer the namaz all his life.'

The Caliph of Baghdad, the senior, middle and junior ministers and other luminaries accompanied Suhrawardi to welcome Bahauddin. Kissing his feet, Suhrawardi said, 'You will stay in our city, won't you?'

— No.

— But why not?

— This city has become wayward. Your Caliph has turned it into a kingdom of pleasure.

Touching Bahauddin's feet, the Caliph said, 'Will you see another city like Baghdad anywhere in the universe, Shaikh?'

— Is this what Allah wanted? Is this what Nabi wanted?

— The world doesn't remain unchanged, Shaikh.

— How much do you know of the world? Bahauddin roared. — You've turned Baghdad into a bazaar.

— Is life possible without a marketplace, Shaikh? The Caliph smiled.

— What do you know of life? Do you know what the word Caliph means?

— You insult me, Shaikh.

— You deserve to be insulted.

— And why is that?

— Don't you know that the path of Islam is not one of wanton pleasure? Let me tell you a story then. A religious scholar was wandering about on the roads and markets, holding a lamp. Someone came up to ask him, 'Why do you need a lamp in daylight?' The scholar said, 'I'm looking for a human being.' The man laughed. 'So many people around you, can't you see any of them?' After a pause the ulema said, 'I'm looking for a real human being, beneath whose feet I want to live like the earth.' That's not the kind of Caliph you are. Your Baghdad only chases money and people.

— Must everyone remain impoverished forever, Shaikh?

— What do you mean by poverty? Do you mean starvation? Do you mean homelessness? Do you mean deprivation from riches? Poverty of the soul is the only poverty there is.

— You can tell us all this at the Jama Masjid on Thursday.

Bahauddin burst out laughing. — Is there anyone in your Baghdad who will listen?

Kissing Bahauddin's feet again, Suhrawardi said, 'Say it for my sake at least.'

— Hmm . . . the truth resides beyond crowds of people. I shall speak for your sake, Suhrawardi. Look at that star there . . .

The Caliph smiled. 'You're showing us a star by daylight, Shaikh?'

Bahauddin smiled too. — You'll never be able to see it. Day and night are the same to me. In some other land in the world you can see stars at this moment. Day and night are nothing but the rotation of the sphere. It is day everywhere, night everywhere.

The Caliph laid out all his gifts at Bahauddin's feet. Touching his feet again, he said, 'I shall be gratified if you accept my humble offerings.'

— Why should I take all this? I do not accept whatever I cannot take with me to Allah. Take these back. Turning to Suhrawardi, Bahauddin said, 'Have you not taught the Caliph some tact? A copy of the Quran made by an artist is far more valuable to me than this wealth.'

Now listen to what happened after the afternoon namaz on Thursday. From the Caliph downwards, every single one of Baghdad's eminent people was present. Shaikh Bahauddin would speak on the poverty of the soul. The fluttering of the pigeons' wings could be heard in the compound of the mosque. As soon as Bahauddin stood up, all sounds ceased.

Bahauddin stood in silence for a long time. Eventually his eyes grew blurred with tears. He began to speak. 'If all the trees in the world were words written down, and all the seas were ink, and if there were seven oceans even after this, what Allah has to say will never end. He is victorious, knowledgeable. Have you not seen that Allah brings night in the daytime and day at night? It is on his authorization that the sun and the moon follow their timetables. Allah alone knows of Judgement Day, he sends rain, he alone knows what lies in the womb. You do not know whether you will earn money tomorrow, nor do you know where you will die. Only he knows, Allah.

'That I am here today to talk about the poverty of the soul is itself a symptom of that poverty. Had I been free of it I would not have been here to address you. Do you know what poverty of the soul is like? To the sick man's tongue, even what is sweet tastes bitter. Do you know what poverty of the soul is like? It is like a barren womb. Let me tell you a story. A qissa can tell more than a thousand words of philosophy. Philosophies come and philosophies go, but a story lives on for thousands of years, in different lands, in different forms. This story is about Karim. His wife's name was Anar. They'd been married ten years, but still they didn't have any children. Karim loved his wife so much that he never considered divorcing her for not having a baby. On a friend's advice, Karim took his wife to the doctor. The doctor heard them out, examined Anar, and then sat there in silence.

— What's your diagnosis, Hakim sahib? Karim asked.
— Very sad, very sad. The doctor shook his head.
— What's wrong with my wife?

— There's nothing more that I can do, Karim bhai.
— Why not?
— It's very sad. Your wife will be in her grave within forty days.

Anar slumped to the floor, unconscious, when she heard this. Karim managed to bring her home somehow. She gave up the routine of her daily life altogether. Can anyone lead a normal life in the face of death? Soon Anar stopped eating.

Bahauddin lapsed into a long silence. 'And then?' asked the Caliph.

— Infidel! Bahauddin screamed.
— Shaikh! Suhrawardi shrieked.
— Why are these illiterate people here at this majlis, Shaikh Suhrawardi? They do not even know the etiquette of listening to a story? Does the Caliph need a shit that he interrupts me? Bahauddin burst into laughter.

The Caliph stood up. 'Why do you keep humiliating me?'

— So that the barren woman can have a child.
— Am I a woman?
— You do not even understand figures of speech. How did you become a Caliph? Listen to the story. Forty days passed, but Anar did not die. Karim ran to the doctor.

The doctor chuckled. 'I knew it. Your wife will have a baby now.'

— How?
— She had become too fat. That was why she could not conceive. She gave up eating, didn't she?
— She did.

— Your wife wouldn't have stopped eating except on the fear of death. Nor would she have become thinner. When people start thinking of the Day of Judgement they clean up their lives. Your wife is absolutely fine now. Don't worry, Karim bhai, you will be a father soon. Don't forget my kebab and paratha when you do.

Laughing, Bahauddin said, 'Karim and Anar had a child within the year. Listen to me, Caliph, Baghdad has become obese. The obesity of wealth. Unless you can shed this weight there will be no children. It is this fat that is the poverty of Baghdad's soul.'

A few days later, as Bahauddin's caravan was leaving Baghdad, news came of the Mongols' invasion of Balkh, which had been reduced to ruins, a city of the dead. Clasping Jalal to his breast, Shaikh Bahauddin muttered, 'There will be no home for us anywhere in the world anymore. We have become refugees, Jalal.'

There, you can see Shaikh Bahauddin's caravan moving forward. After a long journey they will reach Larende, where they will be given sanctuary by Amir Musa, a navab of the Seljuk kingdom.

NINE

When leaving Baghdad Shaikh Bahauddin had heard that Balkh had died. Twelve thousand mosques had been destroyed, fourteen thousand copies of the Quran burnt, fifteen thousand scholars and students at different madrassas killed, two hundred thousand men slaughtered. Bahauddin had smiled in his head. This was how the Mongols had left their names in the history books. You never knew how people became part of history. Some were driven mad by the lust for blood, others by love. What value did the history of mankind have in the context of the universe, wondered Bahauddin. But it wasn't possible to tell anyone all this while being swept away like refugees. And so the days passed one at a time, and Bahauddin became used to talking to himself. Talk to yourself, Baha, there's no one here to listen to you.

— Baha . . .
— What?
— What's on your mind, Baha?
— Where does this road end?

— You are a traveller on an endless road.
— I cannot bear the weight of eternity, Lord.
— Eternity is very light, Baha.
— Then why is it a burden? Why does my back bend under it?
— You have amassed much knowledge.
— What shall I do, Lord?
— Discard the burden by the side of the road.

On the way to Larende, Bahauddin burst into laughter one day. — Throw it away, throw it all away.

The caravan came to a halt. Bahauddin sat down by the side of the road, tearing out clumps of his hair and beard and shouting, 'Throw it away, throw it all away.'

Many years later, Maulana told his disciple, 'No one but I could understand Shaikh Bahauddin's self-destructive cries. He had no home anymore once he had left Balkh. A man's life isn't complete without a home of his own, Hussam.'

A time comes in a person's life when the stories are lost. Events follow in quick succession, like a blizzard of snow. Shaikh Bahauddin arrived at Larende. The Navab built him a new madrassa. Bahauddin lived seven years here, witness to two deaths, a marriage, and two births. Bahauddin's wife Momina Khatun and eldest son Muhammad Alauddin were the ones to die. Around the same time, Jalaluddin was married to Gauhar Khatun, daughter of Lala Sharafuddin from Samarqand. Within a year Bahauddin was born, whom you will come to know later as Sultan Walad. The next year Alauddin Muhammad was born.

From Larende Shaikh Bahauddin's fame spread everywhere, reaching as far as Konya, the capital of the Seljuk kingdom. At the time, the Seljuk empire was like a house built at twilight. Sultan Alauddin Kayqubad invited Shaikh Bahauddin. It didn't suit a learned man like him to languish in Larende. Come to Konya, let the city be illuminated by the light of the thousand suns of your genius and devotion.

Bahauddin accepted the invitation. Broken within by the destruction of Balkh, he lived only two years more after moving to Konya. Waves of students and others eager for religious understanding would descend on the madrassas and mosques of Konya to hear him talk. Suddenly Shaikh stopped in the middle of his speech. His son and disciple Jalaluddin was standing next to him. The young man whispered, 'What's wrong?'

The father glanced at his son. 'How much more can I talk?'

— Everyone's here to listen to you speak.
— Why?
— Because you are the master.

Shaikh shouted, 'Leave me alone, Jalal. I have said thousands of things over all these years. Still Balkh was destroyed. Do you remember, Jalal, that the Mongols have burnt fourteen thousand copies of the Quran? What purpose has all that I said all these days served? When books are burnt civilizations are destroyed, Jalal. I can hear the crackle of books being burnt.'

Many, many years later Maulana had asked Hussam,

'Do you know what a kitab is, Hussam?'
— Footprints.
— How did you know?
— By seeing yours.
— What do you see in them, Hussam?
— A book comes alive in every single footprint.

Look, Hussam, books are being written on each of Konya's streets. Sceptics had said that books would be lost one day. Is that ever possible, Hussam? This entire world has been created through Allah's script.

Pardon me, my learned readers, I have committed a small error. Had this story been written chronologically, Hussam should not have entered it now. But Maulana and his disciple Hussam keep infiltrating the narrative through gaps. So it is necessary to introduce Hussam to you right now. Questions about him must have risen in your mind too. His name was Hussamuddin Chalabi. He was a Futuwwa Fityan, a member of the youth brigade. His father was the Akhi, or head, of a Futuwwa. Hussam grew to be Maulana Rumi's favourite disciple in a very short span of time, and Maulana later appointed him Caliph of the Maulvi order. It was on Hussam's request that Maulana began composing his epic Masnavi.

Bahauddin died in 1231 AD at the age of eighty-five. He left behind two priceless treasures for the world. His kitab *Ma'arif*, which documented his speeches and sayings, and his son Jalaluddin, who was to gradually be transformed into Maulana Rumi in the hands of the invisible cook.

Jalal was twenty-four at the time of Shaikh Bahauddin's

death. The calm, dignified, young man's learning and his uncompromising pursuit of the Sufi way had begun to be talked about far beyond Konya. Jalal began to teach in his father's madrassa. This was when Syed Burhanuddin al-Tirmidhi arrived in Konya. He was visiting the city to enquire after the health of his teacher Shaikh Bahauddin. Learning of the Shaikh's demise, he broke down like a tree uprooted by a storm, although he did recover within a day or two. This was no time to collapse, he told himself, for Maulana-e Buzurg's death has cast a huge responsibility on me. Who else but he could perform the duty of escorting Jalal on the correct path to devotion? It was he who used to teach Jalal as a child in Balkh.

One day he called Jalal to his side. 'I have some things to tell you.'

— Let us sit in the library.

— Yes, I've heard Maulana-e Buzurg preferred to spend most of his time in it.

— Yes. The Sultan gifted him this library. Jalal sat in silence for some time. Then he said in a voice tinged with memories, 'As afternoon declined towards evening, he would sit in his library every day. He loved the smell of the library at that hour. I won't leave Konya, Jalal, he would tell me. Where else will I find a library such as this? Where else in the world is there a smell like this?

— What kind of smell?

Shaikh Bahauddin sat for a long time with his eyes closed. Then he whispered, 'The fragrance of lost perfume.'

— What kind of perfume?

— The perfume made from the navel of a musk deer that died long, long ago.

— When did it die?

Shaikh Bahauddin had not answered.

Entering the library, Syed Burhanuddin asked, 'Do you get the same smell, Jalal?'

— No, I don't.

— But you must. You are the inheritor of Shaikh's legacy, unless the same smell comes to you your life will be wasted. I have decided to stay in Konya for the time being.

— Do you think I'd have let you go? That you are here after Shaikh's death is on the Lord's instructions.

Burhanuddin embraced Jalal. There was a pattern of tears on Jalal's face.

— Why do you weep, Jalal?

— Why did he leave me alone?

— No, Jalal, this does not befit you. What has Maulana-e Buzurg taught us? To be alone. We are all journeying towards the wedding night. Only through solitude shall we be united with love. Alone like Majnu, when he has himself become Laila. But now to business.

— Tell me what I should do.

— Jalal, I want you to be just like our Shaikh. I want to see you as a complete man. Shaikh has placed this responsibility on me.

— I shall do as you ask me.

— You have to acquire much more knowledge. For this you will have to go to Aleppo and Damascus.

— As you wish.

Syed Burhanuddin set off with Jalal. As far as I recollect, it was 1233 AD. Sending Jalal on to Aleppo, Burhanuddin stayed back at Kayseri. After completing his studies in Aleppo, Jalal went to Damascus. As you know, my learned readers, Damascus was the main centre of education, culture and spirituality. Sufi mystics and scholars like Ibn al-Arabi, Uthman al-Rumi, Wahauddin Kirmani and Sadruddin Kunai all lived in Damascus at the time. As far as I know, Jalal met Ibn al-Arabi. Many years later Maulana Rumi had told Hussam, 'I was like a virgin piece of paper then. Still, my conversation with Shaikh Ibn al-Arabi gave me no peace.'

— Why not, Shaikh?

— Our paths were different. He wanted to create a flight of logic to reach Allah, while my way is through a river of tears. His road is the one of knowledge, mine is the one of love.

Jalal's fame in Damascus as a student of philosophy and religion was at its height then. Most of the students congregated around him. One day Jalal had come out of the madrassa, surrounded by friends. An aged, emaciated dervish slumped to the road near his feet. Jalal bent to help him up.

— Who are you?

The dervish laughed. — All the accounts of the world are in your hands. Can you support me a minute?

The dervish took Jalal's hands and kissed them. Jalal withdrew his hands slowly. The dervish gazed at him in deep concentration for some time before walking off in the opposite direction.

Much later Rumi had told Hussam, 'He was laughing loudly as he walked away. Do you know what he was saying, Hussam?'

— What?

— This fellow has not been cooked yet. Wait, my friend, we shall meet again.

Fifteen years later, when the same dervish was over sixty, he caught a glimpse of Jalal again on a road in Konya. I shall tell you all these stories later, my learned readers. Completing his studies in Damascus, Jalal went to Syed Burhanuddin's home in Kayseri.

— You will now have to observe the Chillah, the days of penance and solitude.

— As you command.

— You'll have to spend three periods of forty days each alone. A hundred and twenty days. Can you do it?

— By Shaikh's and your grace, I can.

After a hundred and twenty days of solitude, Jalal emerged a gaunt figure. 'What do you see, Jalal?' Burhanuddin asked him.

'This world is shrouded in fog,' Jalal muttered.

— What sort of fog?

— Of love. Why do I want to weep, Shaikh?

— Silence, roared Burhanuddin. There was only one Shaikh, Shaikh Bahauddin. Do not address me as 'Shaikh'.

— What shall I do now?

— You will teach, you will guide people along the path of devotion.

— You will be by my side, won't you?

— Let me take you to Konya.
— You must be with me. Jalal gripped his arm.
— No, Jalal. It's time for me to leave.
— Why?

Syed Burhanuddin laughed. — A lion from Tabriz is coming to Konya. You know I'm a lion too, Jalal. Can two lions coexist? It is necessary for the lion of Tabriz to enter your life now. And so I must leave. Goodbye.

TEN

The person who returned from Damascus was no longer Jalaluddin Balkhi, but Maulana Rumi. However, he was already being addressed as Maulana before going to Aleppo and Damascus. And his father was Maulana-e Buzurg, the greatest Maulana. Rumi was much thinner now, which was why he appeared even taller. His body held the glow of yellow leaves shed in early spring. A new madrassa was established in the front half of the house. He was thirty-six. Four hundred pupils came to his madrassa every day for an education. They included renowned scholars, noblemen, and even the Sultan of Konya. None of them had ever met such an extraordinary teacher. He explained the essentials of life and the world through stories. He walked slowly, perpetually sunk in thought. At the madrassa or the mosque, on Konya's roads or at the baths, whenever anyone asked him a question he listened with bowed head, answered, adding with a smile, 'What I say is not the last word, however.' But it was, to everyone in Konya. As though Maulana

Rumi was uttering the words of Allah, just like Nabi.

There are a couple of things I have not told you, my learned readers. Maulana's first wife Gauhar Khatun died before he left for Aleppo and Damascus. Maulana's second wife was Kira Khatun. As far as I know, Kira was of Greek origin. She bore Maulana two more children— Muzaffaruddin Amir Alim Chalabi and Malika Khatun. Al Mustasimi told me that Kira Khatun's beauty was like an ancient willow's, uninhibited and understated at the same time.

On his return from Damascus, Maulana discovered three youthful soulmates. Hussamuddin Chalabi, the young Greek Thereanos, and his own eldest son Sultan Walad. All of them were in their twenties then.

One day, with all the students at the madrassa having gone home, and only the three young men sitting in front of himself, Maulana handed a copy of the *Attarnama* to Hussam, saying, 'Open the book to any page and read me the first two words, Hussam.'

As soon as Hussam had uttered these words Maulana Rumi held up a hand to stop him. Shutting his eyes, he flawlessly recited all that was written on the page, followed by an explanation. Touching his feet, Sultan said, 'What is it, Maulana?'

— He's coming, Sultan.
— Who?
— He's in Konya.
— Whom are you talking about?
— Hussam . . .

— Yes, Maulana?

— Describe Konya in winter.

— The houses, roads, trees, are all hidden beneath snow, Maulana. Nothing but white everywhere.

— It's so cold, Hussam. The travellers are confined to their inns. No road to any part of the world is open. Only the ravens can be heard cawing all winter. After this there will be spring, isn't that so, Hussam?

— Yes, Maulana. The rose will bloom. The nightingale will sing for it. They'll meet after such a long time.

Maulana smiled. — You people only talk of the nightingale. Aren't you going to mention the heron? It dons a white robe to visit Mecca every year. Do you know where it builds its nest, Sultan?

— On the tower of the mosque.

— The soul of the heron has arrived in Konya, Sultan. Spring is here.

— Who is he?

— You will see him very soon.

— Where?

— On the streets of this very town. He is waiting for me.

— Do you know him?

— No. Shaikh Burhanuddin had told me that a lion would arrive from Tabriz.

— But you said it was the soul of the heron.

— All melded together, Sultan. He is the lion, he is the soul of the heron, he is the rose's lover, the nightingale.

— Do you know him, Hussam asked.

— No, Hussam.

Maulana Rumi entered his library. Since his return from Damascus, Maulana had spent most of his time in this favourite room of Shaikh Bahauddin's. He was engrossed in his father's book *Ma'arif*. All this time he had considered Shaikh Bahauddin nothing but a religious scholar, but as he read *Ma'arif*, the life of a passionate devotee was being unveiled to him. He did not know that Shaikh loved poetry. There were nearly thirty fragments of verse in *Ma'arif*. It was no longer possible to distinguish between Shaikh's own lines and those that he had gleaned from other people. In one of the poems he had referred to himself as Allah's lover. Just like the lover who composes poetry for his beloved, Shaikh too had written these verses for the Lord. All our praises for our beloved's features and eyes and lashes are actually encomiums to Allah. In his library, Maulana Rumi discovered a lover of beauty and poetry in Bahauddin.

In *Ma'arif* Bahauddin had repeatedly exhorted people to stay away from all manner of filth in the world. According to him, there were four kinds: educated people, cities, armed forces, and rulers. O inhabitants of the world, do not allow your hearts to be covered in grime. The fire in an oven blackens everything at first, then reddens them, and finally whitens. In the same way, the flames of Allah's love take us from black to red and finally to the purity of white.

Maulana sensed a strange, raging storm within himself today, taking him out of the world of *Ma'arif*. He became even more restless over the next few days. He would lapse into silence during his discourses, gazing out of the window. It seemed to Hussam that his eyes saw nothing at all.

One day his son Sultan Walad went into the ladies' chambers to tell Kira Khatun what was happening. Just as Maulana loved Sultan, Sultan too was duty-bound to his father. Unable to bear Maulana's agitation, he was hoping that Kira's company would calm his father down. His Greek stepmother was so beautiful that even Sultan felt tempted sometimes. At other times she appeared similar to the Virgin Mary. Maulana too was apprehensive about Kira's loveliness, and seldom allowed her out of the house.

Kira came to the library late that same evening. As always, Maulana was astonished to see her. Once again he felt that she was not of this world, that she had come from an invisible universe somewhere else, as someone, as a poet of the future would write, who visited but once, never to be seen again.

— You here, Bibijaan? Maulana took Kira's hand.

— I haven't seen you in a long time, Maulana. You never visit us anymore. I'm told you're always in the library.

— Hmm . . . Come.

— Don't you feel the urge to see me anymore, Maulana?

— Of course I do. I do see you, Kira. In my dreams.

Kira began to laugh like a mad woman. Maulana was transfixed by her beauty and laughter.

The laughter stopped suddenly. Kissing her husband's feet, Kira said, 'I beg your pardon, Maulana. I should not have asked this question. Nor do I know why I laughed. Forgive me, Maulana.'

Maulana sat down next to Kira, putting his hand on her back he said, 'You know I never lie, Kira.'

— Don't embarrass me, Maulana.

— Let me speak, Kira.

— I beg your pardon.

— I wanted you to call me by my name Jalal at least once, Kira. But I have been your Maulana too from the very first day. Sometimes I wonder if I had not been Maulana-e Buzurg's son, let's say if I had owned a carpet shop or a perfumery in Konya's market, or even sold baskets on the road, you and I could have lived as easily as other couples do. This existence of mine has not allowed me a taste of easy living. That is why I see you in my dreams, Kira, I lie with you every night here in this library, it's just the two of us.

— What's all this you're saying, Maulana?

— Do I seem an infidel to you, Kira?

— Who am I to judge you, Maulana? If I can spend my entire life by your side, that will be Allah's kindness. Will you just answer a single question?

— Yes?

— What's wrong with you? You have been restless for several days.

Maulana smiled. — Sultan must have told you. Or was it Hussam?

— It was Sultan.

— This son of mine loves me so much, it feels like a chain around my neck sometimes.

— He's a favourite of yours too.

— Yes, a deeply religious soul. Not even I am worthy of him.

— What are you saying, Maulana!

— Truly, Kira, I speak from my heart. Sultan can pledge his life to someone he loves. While I am often in a dilemma.

— But what's the matter with you?

— Wait. Maulana rose to his feet. Going with measured footsteps to the door of the library, he locked it. Then he undressed, shedding all his clothes. — Do you recognize me, Kira?

— What are you doing, Maulana? Kira hid her face in her hands.

An unclothed Maulana embraced Kira, who rested her head against her emaciated husband's chest and began to weep.

— Don't cry, Kira. This may be our last night together. A lion from Tabriz has arrived in Konya. He is hiding somewhere. Ever since I had this realization, a fire has been burning within me. He will destroy everything we have. Once the lion reveals itself nothing will be the same, Kira.

Maulana began to take Kira's clothes off, one by one. Making her lie down on the floor of the library, Maulana lay down next to her and whispered, 'Kira . . .'

— Yes?

Like two willow branches Kira's long arms enveloped Maulana.

— What a beautiful garden. A garden in spring.

— Where?

— You, Kira.

— Have you gone mad today, Maulana?

— When I bathe in the warm springs of Meram, it is your body I see, Kira, in the sound of the water whirling around me.

Maulana sat up, made Kira sit on his lap, and placed his lips on her neck. His tongue began to move between Kira's breasts, in the cleavage between them.

Kira too began to play with Maulana's body. Eventually they had intercourse.

Before leaving Kira said, 'Has the fire within you died down, Maulana?'

— Farewell, muttered Maulana.

Kira did not stay another instant.

The next day Sultan asked Kira, 'Did you meet Maulana?'

Kira smiled. — Don't worry, Sultan, he has recovered.

— I knew you alone could help him get better.

— Sultan?

— Yes.

— Can you make arrangements for me to live somewhere else?

— Why? This is your own house.

— Maulana does not need me anymore. I want to live alone now, Sultan.

— Did Maulana say anything?

— No. As I was leaving, he only muttered, farewell. I know how he uses words, Sultan.

— Did he say anything more?

— No, that one word is enough, Sultan. He won't live amongst us anymore.

— Where will he go?

— You love Maulana so much, Sultan, but you don't understand what he says.

Hussam, who was standing at a distance, came up to them to ask, 'Where's Maulana?'

— In his library, answered Kira.

Going to the library, Sultan and Hussam found the door open. Maulana was not inside. After a quick exchange of glances, they waited no more. A little later they were seen rushing along the street. Their search led them to the shop of a butcher selling lamb in the market, where Maulana was sitting. Sultan and Hussam kissed his feet. — Why are you sitting here, Maulana?

— He's here.

— Who's here?

— The lion of Tabriz.

— Come home now. Hussam took his arm.

— All right.

Maulana Rumi returned home slowly, his arms around his companions' shoulders.

ELEVEN

One morning in the library Maulana sent for Sultan. Sultan arrived, kissed Maulana's feet, and looked askance at him. He had not yet mustered the courage to ask what Maulana wanted to say.

— Sultan ...
— Yes.
— He's coming today.
— You're sure?
— My heart says he is.
— Tell me what I should do.
— Take care of everything, Sultan.
— Very well.
— Where are Hussam and Thereanos?
— They'll be here soon.
— Did I tell you something, Sultan?
— What, Maulana?
— Die before you die. Do you know who said this?
— No.
— Shaikh Burhanuddin. It's in the Hadith. Do you

understand what it means, Sultan?

— You tell me, Maulana.

— If you do not die, how will you rise again? You will die and be resurrected in different ways all your life. Today is my day to rise again.

I must tell you about Atabeg now. Atabeg Arsalandogmas. No one knew who this boy was. Where did his name spring from in that case? Asking in Konya's market would have revealed the answer.

Atabeg lived in the market, spending his nights in one shop or another. But who had named him? His parents had abandoned him in the market at birth. Where had his name sprung from, then? Some said there was no reason for surprise, if you've been born you're bound to have a name. Why lose sleep over who named the boy? As long as Konya's market existed, so would Atabeg. What kind of question was this? When Allah sends someone to the world, he sends a name too. All names are his choice.

Some people said as they wandered around the market, 'Atabeg, fine. But Arsalandogmas? Who gave such a name to the bastard?'

It was snowing that winter night. Atabeg was roaming around Konya's silent market alone. He simply couldn't sleep. Pigeons flew about in the central square all day. Who knew where they were now? Why doesn't a single pigeon call me to bed, wondered Atabeg? Why don't they tuck me under their wing and tell me to go to sleep? Walking around the empty market of Konya, Atabeg called out, 'Ma . . . my mother . . . my Paloma . . .'

— Yes, my darling?
— Why did you abandon me in this huge market, Ma?'
— Idiot!

It was like the roar of a lion. Atabeg whirled around and jumped out of his skin. He had seen the old man who had just spoken wandering around Konya's market for the past few days. He appeared to be searching for something constantly. Shaggy, unkempt hair, his moustache and beard a forest. Every time Atabeg's eyes fell on the white-haired, white-bearded man, he looked away in fear. The old man's eyes were blazing.

The man put his hand on Atabeg's shoulder. — Whom are you looking for, you idiot? For your mother? Come to me . . .

The old man knelt on the ground, clasping Atabeg to his chest. — You have no parents, and nor do I. We're both wanderers, aren't we? Come with me, it's madness to walk around in this cold.

— But so were you.

He burst into laughter. — I walk around, I fly around too. 'Isn't that the ancient bird,' says everyone. 'Catch him.' But it's not so easy to catch me. Do you know what the Lord whispered in my ear when I was born? 'Shams, my boy, I didn't bring you into this world to live in a cage.' Come along now . . .

Shams took Atabeg's hand as they started walking. He took the boy to the inn where sugar merchants lived. This was the inn where he had taken shelter on his arrival in Konya. Making a bed for Atabeg, he made the boy lie down and began to tell him stories. Soon Atabeg fell asleep. Shams smiled at the boy, and then looked up at the sky. 'Take your servant's life and give the boy a new one, my Lord.'

Shams sat looking at Atabeg all night. He had once told Rumi, 'Love is actually a prolonged vigil. The long wait for your sleeping lover to awaken while you sit alongside.'

Let us look closely at this old man, my learned readers. He is over sixty. Shamsuddin Tabrizi. People had shortened his name to Shams Tabrizi. His parents had named him Muhammad Malekdad. It is said that the souls of Sufi mystics would fly every night from the western Iranian town of Tabriz to Mecca in the form of red and green doves, circling the Kaaba all night. When Shamsuddin was young there were seventy Sufi dervishes who placed more faith in the awakening of the soul than in knowledge and education. When telling Maulana about Tabriz, Shams had once said, 'It is an incredible, mysterious city, filled with people in comparison to whom I am a mere buoy deposited ashore by the ocean. Just think of them. How impoverished the world is growing now day by day.'

About his father, Shamsuddin said, 'He was a good man, extremely courteous. But being a good man and being Allah's lover are not the same thing.'

When Shams was a child, a shadowy figure had materialized in front of him for a moment before vanishing. Shams gave up his regular life after this incident. One day his father asked him, 'What's the matter, Muhammad?'

— Nothing.

— Why do you look so agitated all the time? You seem distraught. You're not even eating properly.

Muhammad stared at his father for some time. 'Shall I tell you a story?'

— Tell me, my son.

— A hen was trying to make some duck's eggs hatch.

— How peculiar. Muhammad's father smiled. — What happened then?

— One day the eggs did hatch and the ducks tottered out. When they grew a little older they began to swim in the river. The mother hen could only watch from the edge of the water, she didn't know how to swim. All she could do was run up and down the bank.

— What does this story mean?

— I am a duck and you are the hen.

Trembling with rage, Muhammad's father said, 'If this is how you talk with your own people, who knows how you will talk to your enemies.'

— I have neither people of my own, nor enemies.

— What do you mean?

— I'm here to see the world just this one time, Abba.

— Have you gone mad, Muhammad?

— You won't understand me. I don't expect you to, either. We aren't cut from the same cloth, Abba.

That is why Shamsuddin Tabrizi was a mystery, my learned readers. Some used to say that he was an uneducated ascetic who knew all kinds of magic. Others claimed he was another Socrates. As all of you know, unrestrained passion, extreme poverty and a violent death were what fate held in store for Socrates. Shamsuddin appeared a similar figure to me. Nothing but a thirst for something he was seeking, though he himself did not know what it was. But he was convinced that one day he would find the flintstone which he could rub to turn life into a sacred flame. That was why Shams would scream without warning, weep like a torrential downpour, or spit on 'infidels' while speaking. Who were these infidels? Those who were imprisoned in cages of knowledge, who did not know Majnu. It was in search of his personal Majnu that Shams had set forth from Tabriz one day. Baghdad, Damascus, Aleppo, Kayseri, Sivas, Erzurum, Erzinkan—he visited many different places, spent many hours in the company of holy men, and still told the sky every night, 'And yet my heart is not fulfilled, my Lord.'

You will recognize Shamsuddin, the Sun of Tabriz, from a story or two about the company of holy men. In Damascus, Shams became the disciple of Ibn Arabi. Some say that Maulana Rumi and Ibn Arabi were the two trailblazers of Sufi mysticism. One of them walked the path of love and the other, of logic and philosophy. Ibn Arabi was born in Espanha in 1165 AD, twenty years before Shams's birth. He used to address Shams as 'my son', while Shams considered him a giant. And yet he felt that Ibn Arabi did not walk the path of the prophet. Much later he had told Maulana Rumi, 'I learnt a great deal from Ibn Arabi, but it cannot be compared to what I got from you. Can a pebble be compared to a pearl, Maulana?'

In Baghdad there was a famous Sufi mystic named Wahaduddin Kirmani. I'm told he met Maulana Rumi too.

Maulana did not care for Kirmani. One night Shams saw Kirmani gazing at a pot of water.

— What are you looking at, Shaikh? Shams asked.
— The moon.
— Where is it?

Kirmani smiled. 'In this pot, my son.'

— Have you sprained your neck?
— Why do you ask?
— Why aren't you looking at the moon in the sky?

Kirmani smiled again. 'You won't understand, my son.'

Shams left Baghdad the same day. Kirmani may have been a famous mystic, but Shams did not need him on his own journey of devotion.

Famous. Shams had begun to suspect and despise this word. Fame was actually a collection of misconceptions about a person. Shams set himself on a road of concealment. I am nobody, just a wasted man. I am an oyster, Allah, a mere drop you have drawn.

It was in Damascus that Shams had the first dream. Wandering around the city, he kept saying in his head, 'Let me meet your closest friend but once, Lord.'

One night he heard in his dream, 'Do not worry, you shall be united with him.'

— Where is he?
— In Anatolia, in the kingdom of Rome, which is why his name is Rumi, my son.
— When will I meet him, my Lord?
— It is not time yet. You will meet him when the time is right.

That was why Shams had laughed loudly on seeing Maulana Rumi in Damascus, saying, 'He hasn't been cooked yet. Wait, my friend, we shall meet again.'

Shamsuddin searched for Allah's closest friend everywhere. He had no choice but to seek shelter somewhere at night. At that time one's profession and social status determined where one would sleep. The merchants would put up at caravanserais, the maulanas at madrassas, and mystics at the Dervish Inn, which was free. But Shamsuddin always slept at a caravanserai, so that he wasn't recognized as a dervish. However, he needed money to stay and eat at the caravanserai. Where was he to get money? Why, just teach children the Quran. Shams had discovered a technique to teach the entire Quran in three months. Whenever he stayed in a city for a long time, this was how he made a living. As for short stays, he would stitch and mend clothes and even shoes. As a young man he had actually worked as a mason. All of this with just one objective. Conceal yourself. No one should recognize you. You're worthless. You have only one task, to find the Lord's closest friend. After that you could go to your grave in peace. You have to pay to see the world before you can leave.

Look, Atabeg is mumbling in his sleep. The aged Shamsuddin is leaning over him. He shakes the boy gently, and Atabeg opens his eyes. The feeble sunlight of winter has entered the room.

— Atabeg.

Atabeg sits up with a start. — Yes, huzoor?

— There's only one Huzoor, Atabeg. I am your friend.

— Yes. Atabeg's eyes sparkle. The fire that he has seen in the old man's eyes all these days had now been extinguished, leaving only a benign blue flame.

— Come, we must go now.

— Where?

— On our travels. I shall meet him today.

— Meet whom?

Embracing Atabeg, Shamsuddin said, 'The one I have been looking for all these years. I was looking for you too, Atabeg. I have found you. But I haven't found him yet.'

TWELVE

We seldom know exactly when a character who has never been mentioned earlier infiltrates a story. The boy named Atabeg Arsalandogmas also stole in this way, my learned readers. He may have no existence in history. But to me, Ibn Battuta, he is so very real. When and in which land did I hear such names? What made me think he is Greek? There are no answers to such questions. I only felt the presence of a young boy wandering about in this story, seeing everything, questioning everything. Do you not feel that as Shamsuddin walked along holding Atabeg's hand, it was his own childhood he was leading by the hand? The day our childhood leaves us is the day we will die.

All morning Atabeg and Shamsuddin kept walking, through wide avenues, narrow roads, and dingy lanes. Atabeg asked, 'Where do you live?'

— Very far away.
— Where?
— In Tabriz.
— How far is it to Tabriz?

Shamsuddin laughed. — As far as your heart is from mine.

Atabeg laughed too. — You talk like a lunatic.

— That's what my father used to say too. Now here you are, echoing him.

— I'm hungry. Atabeg tugged at the sleeve of Shamsuddin's tattered robe.

— Let's go. How will you get any food unless we go to the market?

It was almost time for the afternoon namaz. Everyone was on their way to the Jama Masjid. Entering a kebab shop in the market, Shams ordered parathas and a meat soup for Atabeg. Suddenly the Maulvi's azaan was heard from the minaret of the Jama Masjid. 'Won't you offer the namaz?' asked a round-eyed Atabeg.

— Nonsense. Eat first, you can worry about the namaz later.

Even after the namaz had ended, Shams remained sitting inside the shop with Atabeg. The boy kept badgering him to take him somewhere else. Finally an annoyed Shams said, 'You idiot! Didn't I tell you I'm going to meet him today?'

— Meet whom?

— Shut up. Shams clamped his hand over Atabeg's mouth. Suddenly, Shams said 'He's coming,' and raced away.

The owner of the kebab shop chased him and held him from the back. — Who'll pay for the kebabs?

— The Lord.

— The Lord? Are you playing games with me? Out with

the money. The owner threw himself at Shams. Atabeg caught up with them and began to hit the attacker from behind.

The madrassa of the handloom merchants was close by. Emerging from it, Maulana Rumi mounted a mule. He was surrounded on all sides by students. The kebab shop owner was beating up Shams, who was on the ground, while Atabeg had thrown himself at the shopkeeper, screaming. Arriving at the scene, Maulana Rumi dismounted from his mule, grasping Shams by his arms and helping him to his feet. Shams was both excited and embarrassed at the sight of Maulana. It was him! The person whom he had seen in Damascus fifteen years ago when Allah had not yet cooked him in his kitchen. But now? Shams stared at Maulana. The peas were being boiled in the pot as usual. Waiting to be cooked soon. Has the object of my quest finally appeared in my presence, my Lord?

— What is it, asked Maulana.

The shop owner said obsequiously, 'Huzoor, this gentleman ordered parathas and a soup for the boy. But when it was time to pay, he said he had no money.

— I'll pay.

— Very well, huzoor.

As soon as Maulana walked back to his mount, Shamsuddin screamed, 'Who are you? Why will you pay off my debt?'

— I am Maulana Jalaluddin Rumi. That's the name by which people in Konya address me. Actually my name is Jalaluddin Balkhi. I was born in Balkh, you see. I do not have the power to pay off anyone's debt. I will merely pay for the food.

Shams smiled. 'Will you pay off our entire debt to Allah?'

— It's the Lord's will. Whatever he wants will take place.

— May I ask a question, then? Shamsuddin clamped his hand on Maulana Rumi's shoulder.

Meanwhile the students had ringed around Maulana. Who was this mad man who had sprung from nowhere to question their teacher? Did he not know who Maulana Rumi was and how he was regarded by everyone in Konya, including the Sultan? They were keen to have Maulana remount his mule so that they could escort him home. Maulana kept standing, and said, 'Ask what you have to.' He appeared neither to be waiting nor to be agitated, speaking as a cuckoo does when responding to the silent call of spring.

Pointing to Atabeg, Shams said, 'Do you know this boy?'

— No.

— Why don't you?

— I've never seen him.

— His name is Atabeg. His parents are dead, Maulana. He wanders around on the streets of Konya. The roads are his home, he gets a meal when someone gives him food, he doesn't eat if they don't. I know he doesn't steal. A boy who walks around the city roads on winter nights can never be a thief. Haven't you ever seen him?

— No.

Shams burst into laughter. 'What sort of Maulana are you? A Maulana for whom?'

There was an uproar among the students. Who was this vagabond who dared insult their Maulana in public?

Shams walked off in the opposite direction, holding Atabeg by the hand. Maulana blocked his way. 'You didn't ask your last question, though.'

— That's true. But your students think I am belittling you.

— The question comes before everything else. Ask.

Putting his hand on Maulana's shoulder, Shams said, 'I have wandered this earth all these years just for you, Maulana.'

— The question is essential to confirm whether I am indeed that person.

— The Lord be praised. Shams smiled. 'Bayazid or Muhammad? Which of them do you consider greater, Maulana?'

Much later Maulana had told Hussam, 'This single question took me to the sky beyond the sky.'

— What was your answer, Maulana?

— I stood in silence for a long time, for I had no answer. Then someone seemed to speak from within me, saying, 'Nabi. Muhammad.'

— Why? Why? Shams asked in a frenzy.

— Bayazid's thirst was quenched with a single drop of water. That was as much as he could hold. But Nabi's thirst was infinite. As soon as one thirst was quenched a new one arose. Hazrat's other name is 'thirst'. One day Bayazid felt he had reached the truth, after which he did not look in any other direction. And Muhammad pursued

123

a divine radiance every moment of every day, saying, it will never be possible for me to know you the way you should be known, Lord of the Universe.

As Maulana Rumi spoke, Shams slumped to the ground, unconscious. Mounting his mule, Maulana told his son Sultan and favourite student Hussam, 'Make sure he is not uncomfortable, bring him home.'

All this was a long time ago, my learned readers. I have heard many other legends in Konya about this meeting between Maulana Rumi and Shamsuddin. It is impossible to distinguish between truth and fable now. It is fascinating how the storms of life turn truths and falsehoods upside down. There was a story I heard at a shop selling food in Konya's market. I used to visit it every other day for the taboos seekh kebab. I've already told you about this kebab, which is made by marinating turkey meat for a long time in a mixture of milk, onions, olive oil, tomato juice, salt, and pepper.

Whether you believe this story or not is up to you. One day Maulana was discussing the principles of religion with his students in his library when a deranged Shams appeared. Looking at the books, he said, 'What's all this?'

'You won't understand,' said Maulana with a smile.

You won't believe this, but I'll tell you anyway, a fire broke out in the library at once. Maulana shrieked, 'What's going on? How did a fire start?'

Laughing, Shams said, 'You won't understand either, you fool.' He left the library without waiting another moment.

Many slim books about Maulana Rumi are available in

the markets of Konya. The story I am about to tell you was in one of them. Maulana Rumi was sitting by a waterfall one day, with several books scattered before him. Suddenly the decrepit, frenzied mystic came up to Maulana, asking, 'What's in these books?'

Maulana smiled at him. 'You won't understand. All this is beyond the extremities of your knowledge.'

— Do not be arrogant, shouted Shams.

Maulana smiled again. — How is it possible for everyone to understand everything?

— Really?

Levelling a long look at Maulana, Shams flung the books into the water one by one. Maulana didn't stop him, only saying, 'What have you done? Some of these books are no longer available, my father had given them to me.'

Then a miracle took place. Dipping his hand in the water, Shams retrieved all the books. None of them was wet or ruined. Maulana asked in wonder, 'How is this possible?'

Shams smiled. 'It's possible. This is called divine power, Maulana. You know nothing about this.'

There's yet another story I heard in Konya. Maulana was teaching his students in his madrassa when a halva-seller passed, advertising his wares loudly. Maulana called him in. Lowering his box of halva from his head, the seller gazed at Maulana.

— Well? Give us some of your halva, said Maulana.

The halva-seller handed him some and left the madrassa at once. When he had eaten the halva, Maulana grew restless and went out in search of the halva-seller. Years passed. Maulana did not return. Meanwhile his students had set off in different directions to look for him, but Maulana was not to be found.

Maulana returned on his own a few years later. He no longer spoke to anyone, only writing poetry in Persian from time to time. His students copied the poems, which were ultimately collected in his famous Masnavi.

But who was this halva-seller? Was it Shamsuddin of Tabriz, then? The funny thing is, nowhere in this story is Shams mentioned. But the story of Maulana's life cannot be written without Shams. So, my learned readers, let us return to the first tale.

Maulana Rumi rode his mule towards his house. A single question whirled in his mind—who was this aged dervish? He felt as though spring had arrived in the depths of winter. He muttered:

> *The soul of the heron is at your door today: spring is here. Where are you hiding?*
> *Look, the world has adorned itself with leaves and flowers and roses.*

Meanwhile, Sultan, Hussam and Thereanos put the unconscious Shams on another mule and proceeded home slowly. Atabeg accompanied them. Sultan asked Hussam, 'Have you seen this dervish earlier?'

— Never.

— I cannot even imagine someone challenging Maulana, said Thereanos.

— Is he the one who was supposed to come, said Sultan to himself.

— Who? Hussam placed his hand on Sultan's shoulder.

— Maulana told me this morning, he's coming today.

— Does Maulana know him?

— No.

Suddenly Atabeg said, 'Dadajaan had also said he would be meeting him today.'

— Meeting whom? Sultan noticed Atabeg for the first time. — Who are you?

— Atabeg, he said with a smile.

— Where do you live?

— Nowhere.

— Your parents?

— I haven't any.

Sultan took his hand. — Do you know this dervish?

— No, huzoor. He told me stories last night and put me to sleep. And then he tells me this morning, I'm meeting someone today, come, let's go to the market.

— What stories?

— I don't remember. I fell asleep. When will Dadajaan wake up?

— Soon.

— I'll go as soon as he wakes up, said Atabeg timidly.

— Where will you go? Sultan scooped Atabeg up in his arms.

Atabeg did not answer.

Planting kisses on his cheeks and forehead, Sultan said, 'You will stay at Maulana's house, Atabeg. You're my brother today onwards.'

Atabeg smiled. 'Brother?' he said, widening his eyes.

Sultan realized that the word held no meaning for Atabeg. Since he had no parents, his life did not include brothers or sisters either. As they walked along, Sultan asked, 'Do you know who your father is?'

— Who?

— Maulana Jalaluddin Rumi.

— Sultan! Hussam spoke harshly.

— What is it, Hussam? Could Maulana not have fathered such a beautiful child? And listen, Atabeg, your mother's name is Kira Khatun.

Slipping out of Sultan's arms, Atabeg put his hand on Shamsuddin's inert body on the mule. 'When will Dadajaan wake up?' he asked again.

— Very soon. As soon as we return home and take care of him, he will wake up.

Sultan found Maulana standing outside the front door, looking worried. He asked Maulana, 'Were you talking of this holy man's arrival this morning?'

— I don't know.

Sultan bent to kiss his father's feet.

THIRTEEN

In Maulana's house, in the neighbourhood, in Konya's markets and roads, there was only one question on everyone's lips: who was this mad ancient dervish whom Maulana escorted into his home with such care? Before Shams disappeared forever, he had told Maulana the story of a calligraphist. The calligraphist had three different styles of writing, using a separate quill for each. Only the calligraphist himself could decipher the first script, which was beyond everyone else. The second one was intelligible to himself and to everyone else. As for the third, leave alone others, he couldn't even read it himself. Telling the story, Shams had burst into laughter, and then said, 'Maulana, I am the third script.'

Then who was Maulana? Shams had told Sultan and Hussam, 'I was looking for him on every street in the world. The Lord had told me in my dream that I would find him in Anatolia. I did find him, Sultan, but I simply cannot fathom this. Every day I find something new in Maulana, something which was not there before.

That's why I cannot understand, try as I might. He is an impossible work of creation. How great our Lord is! One day I shall be gone, Hussam, but do not let yourself be content with Maulana's beauty and wonderful messages. There is much more beyond all this. Try to look for that elusive elixir within Maulana.'

Isn't every epic also written in search of that elusive elixir, my learned readers? Our search makes us live and die in so many different stories. New scenes are born all the time.

Let us now enter the room in the inner chambers of Maulana's house where an unconscious Shams was laid down. A crowd had gathered around the aged dervish. It included both aristocrats and noblemen who often frequented the courts of Emirs and Sultans, and Maulana's disciples and students. Maulana was sitting by Shams, stroking his forehead. His eyes suggested he had unexpectedly found an old, old friend who had been shipwrecked. Now he was only waiting for his lost friend to wake up.

Eventually Shams opened his eyes. Maulana bent over him. The aged mystic raised two trembling hands to hold Maulana's face and kiss his forehead. Then, sitting up and surveying the people around him, he finally settled his eyes on Maulana's. Shams said, 'I have turned the prisoner's cell into a garden, Maulana. If my prison is my garden, just think of its beauty.' Looking around and laughing, he said, 'Do any of you understand what I'm saying?'

The people gathered there exchanged glances with one another, and bowed their heads.

Rising to his feet, Shams roared, 'What is the objective of this life? What is it, tell me? You are noble people, there are kings and scholars and teachers among you, hundreds of degrees, tell me, why does this world exist?'

'Who are you, huzoor?' Maulana asked calmly.

— Quiet! Shams roared again. — Why are all these people here?

— You were ill, so . . .

— I am never ill, Maulana. Don't you know how it feels to be united with your friend after a long time, don't you know the tumult within a man, like the ocean on a full moon night? You alone know. The world survives to serve the Lord. So that two friends can meet. And what do humans believe? That bread and meat are the most important things. That the bakery and the slaughterhouse are the last word.

Maulana's younger son appeared, walked up to Shams, and shouted, 'Who are you to say all this? Who are you?'

— Who are you? asked Shams in a steely voice.

— Alauddin. Maulana is my father.

— You are not a worthy son. Leave the room.

Alauddin looked at his father in surprise, saying, 'Aren't you going to say anything, Maulana?'

— Sultan, a stricken Maulana called out.

— Yes? Sultan came up to Maulana.

Maulana said softly, 'Tell Alauddin to leave. Tell everyone to leave.'

— Very well.

Telling him to come closer, Maulana whispered, 'I told

you, Sultan. He's the soul of the heron. Spring has come to Konya.'

Sultan spoke to everyone in turn. Eventually the room emptied out. Maulana and Shams stood facing each other. Then the door was locked from within. Shams embraced Maulana, muttering, 'The Hadith says this world is a prison to believers. I am astonished, Maulana. I haven't seen a gaol anywhere. Everything is joyful. Even if someone pissed on my hand I would forgive them.'

My learned readers, that same room became the location of forty days of penance and solitude for them. Maulana Rumi entered a period of Chillah with Shamsuddin. Maulana's disciples and students turned up thrice a day, but the door to the Chillah khanah did not open. The pupils lost hope with each passing day. How could a genius like Maulana forget everyone else for the sake of a stranger? Students who had come all the way from Baghdad, Samarqand, Farghana and Dilli were about to return home.

Occasionally Alauddin was heard screaming, 'Break the door down and drag the old bugger out. An infidel, a magician.'

Trying to calm his brother down, Sultan would say, 'Everything will be all right, Ala. Have patience.'

One day Kira emerged from her mahal too, asking Sultan, 'Who is this man, my son?'

— I don't know, Ammijaan.

— Some old man who wandered in from the streets. Don't I mean anything to Maulana?

— Ammijaan . . .

— I want to see what's going on.

Kira banged on the door. There was no sound. After she had banged on the door thrice, a faint voice emerged. 'Who is it?'

— Maulana! Kira shrieked, fainting.

Hussam saw Kira lying unconscious outside the door to the penance chamber that day. She was holding a bouquet of unknown flowers, which had never been seen in Anatolia.

'What happened in there, Ammijaan?' asked Sultan.

— Through a crack in the door I saw not two but six more people, surrounding them. They left after offering the namaz, leaving this bunch of flowers at Maulana's feet.

— How did you get them?

— Maulana gave them to me himself.

— When?

— I don't know. Putting her arms around Sultan, Kira burst into tears.

— Didn't Maulana say anything to you?

— He did.

— What did he say?

— He said, these flowers have come from India. Don't tell anyone.

Kira Khatun died nineteen years after Maulana's death. In Konya they would say that the flowers had remained fresh till her death. When sick people came to her, Kira would just touch their body with a single petal and they would recover.

After Maulana's death Hussamuddin Chalabi had

recounted yet another incident. — One day I was peeping through a crack in the door. Maulana was immersed in a book, while Shaikh Shamsuddin was pacing up and down, mumbling to himself. Suddenly he asked, 'What are you reading, Maulana?'

— *Ma'arif*.

Shaikh laughed. — Throw it away, throw away that book. Shaikh Bahauddin's book, isn't it? Throw it away. There's nothing in there.

— What should I do then?

— Don't say a word, Maulana. Not one word.

Hussam wrote of yet another incident he had had a glimpse of. Cupping Maulana's face in his hands, Shaikh kissed his forehead, saying, 'You are a man of so much beauty, Maulana.'

— You are beautiful too, Maulana said.

Shaikh Shamsuddin smiled. 'I am beautiful, but extremely ugly too. You have not seen my ugly side, Maulana. I shall not betray you. You will have to see both my selves: the beautiful and the hideous. In this life that has begun for us, Maulana, there is no pretence, we're both alone.'

Many things changed during those forty days. The students who had come from foreign lands went back home. Since Maulana was not going to be at the madrassa, why should they stay on? Sultan tried to persuade them.

— Please wait a little longer. Maulana will teach you again.

Sultan realized that these students did not love Maulana,

they had congregated only to gather a few scraps of his knowledge.

One day Sultan fetched Kira from her chambers and asked her to peep through the crack in the door.

— What is this I'm seeing, Sultan!

— Yes, Ammijaan. I couldn't believe my own eyes either.

Kira saw Maulana whirling and dancing. His right hand pointed to the sky, and his left, to the floor. He was like the focal point around which circles were being drawn to link the heavens and the earth. Maulana was lost in a whirling dance, like a tornado. And the aged dervish was smiling.

Forty days later the door opened. An old man and a young man stepped out. But it seemed to Kira that her young husband had become much older, gaunt and pale with a thick beard.

— Sultan, called Maulana.

— Yes, Maulana.

— We shall go to the hamam.

— Very well.

— There's only one thing whose absence I have felt over these forty days.

— What is that?

— A bath. Maulana smiled. Taking Shams's hand, he said, 'Come along, Shaikh.'

— Where?

— To the hamam. For a bath.

— I don't care for all that.

— Rule and exception, both of these are duties, Shaikh.

— The Lord be praised.

The old man and the young man undressed and sank into the water at the hamam. Hot and cold streams flowed into the pool at the same time. They bathed each other, embraced and locked themselves in a prolonged kiss.

Hussam's daily journal was available in Konya. I had purchased it. Many people said Hussamuddin Chalabi had written no such journal, that it was the work of an anonymous author who had passed it off as Hussam's. Quite possible. Still I would like to tell you some of the things I read in this counterfeit journal. The real or the fake Hussam had written:

> I am convinced that Shamsuddin and Maulana had entered into a homosexual relationship. Maulana had become his cup-bearer. Despite being the pupil closest to Maulana, I wish to inform you that Maulana had embraced me, kissed me, and kneaded my well-built chest on numerous occasions. Can we conclude that Kira Khatun was unable to satisfy him sexually, then? But it is said that he had intercourse with Kira Khatun eighty times during a single night. This is undoubtedly a fable. Considering the physical state Maulana was in, leave alone eighty times, even eight times would not have been possible. But then everything is the Lord's wish.

I cannot say anything conclusive on this subject, my learned readers. Two individuals had melded with each other, what could be more important than this? Whether it was homosexuality or heterosexuality is irrelevant.

Later, Kira asked Maulana one day, 'What do you see in the old man, Maulana?'

— I had died, Kira. Look, I am alive again.

— Have I not been able to give you anything at all?

— I was a teardrop, now I am a smile. Do you know what he told me?

— What?

— He said, 'You aren't all that mad. How will you stay in this room?' And he said, 'You aren't intoxicated enough. You're still outside the clan.'

— And then?

— I made myself intoxicated, Kira. It was such a joy.

Kira asked with a smile, 'And then he accepted you?'

— No. He said, you have not died yet. You have not become one with the earth in joy. I looked at him with a dead man's eyes. I am still imprisoned, Kira, I am dead, without wings.

Kira embraced Maulana, taking his hand and pressing it on her breasts. Disrobing Kira, Maulana played with them, saying, 'The breasts provide mother's milk to the sons of the earth. And these same breasts are the greatest source of sexual arousal. I consider "breast" a root word.'

— Maulana . . .

— Men have two dead breasts. They will never be able to save this world, Kira. That is why I am leaving you. Shaikh Shamsuddin needs a woman. I want to be at his side to meet his need.

It was a marvellous night. Many such stories wander around the streets of Konya. That night Maulana ran his tongue all over Kira's body as he entered her, after which they left their beds and flew up into the sky. The old men and women of Konya could not sleep that night. The entire sky was covered by a bed laid out for a miraculous sexual union.

Along with the sounds of pleasure spreading across the sky came Maulana's hoarse voice, telling Kira as he kissed her, 'This is what I have been thinking of all day, and I am telling you tonight. Where did I come from, what was I supposed to do? I know nothing. My soul came from an unknown land, Kira, that is where I shall return. My drunken antics began in an inn somewhere. I shall be cured if I can go back there. It is the intervening journey that is sorrowful. I feel as though I am a bird which belongs somewhere else, whose day to fly off is approaching. But who is it who uses my ears to listen? Who speaks with my tongue, Kira? Who sees with my eyes? Do you know what the soul is, Kira? If I had even a fragment of an answer I would leave this jail for the intoxicated. I did not enter of my own free will, Kira, the one who brought me into this world is the one who will take me back home. I am only waiting for him.'

Maulana Rumi's madrassa closed down. He began to sell all the books in his library. Instead of books the room filled with flutes of all kinds and percussion instruments. One day he brought Shams to his empty library. — You shall stay here from now. Do you like it?

— Magnificent! All the garbage of knowledge has vanished.

— But there is someone whom you have forgotten completely.

— Who?

— Atabeg.

— Who is Atabeg?

— Someone who was with you an entire night.

— I see. So many people enter and exit our lives, said Shams dispassionately.

— Atabeg talks of you all the time.

— Let him. Let everyone say whatever they want to. It is just you and I now, Maulana. We do not need anyone else.

Maulana sat in silence. Atabeg's dejected expression played in front of his eyes. Maulana wondered whether this was how Shams had revealed his ugly face.

FOURTEEN

Let us now talk of winter and spring. The story will keep flowing, but if we turn a blind eye to the colours and flavours and aromas with which Konya comes alive in spring, we cannot recognize Maulana. The dazzling festival of earth and sky across Turkistan was known as spring. Many of Maulana's poems are redolent with the fragrance of spring. He starts one of his poems with these lines:

> Look, the violet greets the lily
> While the rose disrobes.

In another poem spring appears to him as Jesus Christ. It's a favourite poem of mine. When you hear it you will understand how spring changes our lives.

> Dinner is over, everyone's asleep. The house is empty.
> We go to the garden, so that the apple and peach can meet
> We bear messages between the rose and the jasmine.

Christ is none other than spring
Removing their shrouds he revives the martyred trees
Uncovered, their grateful mouths seek only kisses
The brightness of the rose and the tulip signifies
The lamps in their hearts. A leaf trembles. I tremble too
In the wind, like Turkish muslin.
The beacon is lit at the tip
This wind is the sacred soul
And the trees, Mary.
See how the husband and wife play hand in hand
And as is the custom at weddings
Pearly waves descend on them from heaven
The scent of Yusuf's garments wafts towards Yaqub.

Yusuf's son-in-law had released his father Yaqub from blindness. Actually spring does bear the scent of Yusuf's clothes. So the days of release from blindness have arrived.

The sun was at the centre of Maulana's life. In every sense. The sun in the sky and the Sun of Tabriz, Shamsuddin. When the sun enters Taurus the earth gets a new life. After a nightlong snowstorm, the rose smiles suddenly in the morning, the green glow of tender grass is seen everywhere, the streets are infused with the heady fragrance of oleaster. Opium, mint, fenugreek and many other shrubs sprout on either side of the waterfall cascading down the hilly slopes of Meram.

I have seen the severe winter of Anatolia. Long, black, despairing days. The roofs covered in snow, thick ropes of ice dangling from buildings, the sun lost from people's lives.

The snow is a symbol of an existence shrouded in darkness, frozen, imprisoned within itself. This was what Maulana was telling his followers as he strolled in Hussam's garden outside the city on a spring day.

— The snow wants to be released too, Hussam. It will not find release until it has melted into water. It is necessary to turn into water, Hussam. It is water that bears the world. Do you know what the snow tells itself? I want to melt, I will become a torrent, and then my journey to the sea begins, that is where my home lies. I cannot take this lonely, hard, dense existence anymore. When will the sword of the sun slice me up? That's the day I will start melting and turn into a current.

Maulana viewed winter another way too. The season is actually the time of retreat, of Khalwa, in the lives of dervishes, when they sit in the darkness to gather their spiritual strength in silence. Like trees. The old leaves from winter will be shed to give birth to new leaves in spring. The dervish will enter the Jilwa stage of the retreat, when Allah's mystery will be revealed to him. The seed concealed in the darkness of the snow-covered earth will germinate.

The raven caws and flies about all winter. He is the representative of the grave. When Cane did not know how to hide his brother Abel's corpse after murdering him, it was the raven who taught him the technique. Is there anyone who doesn't know of the friendship between the world's first murderer—the first one to commit fratricide—and the raven?

The advent of spring marks the end of the raven's

importance, of the memories of killing and burial. The souls of the birds begin their return journey. The nightingale starts singing for his favourite, the rose. The herons arrive too, on their way to their annual pilgrimage to Mecca. Their arrival means that Nauroz, the first day of the year, is coming.

The tribes of Turkistan would pitch their tents around Konya and other towns before the cold season. They spent their lives in the mountains, coming down to the plains only during severe winters. Maulana could be seen walking around their tents sometimes, talking to the mountain people. His son Sultan, Hussam and Thereanos accompanied him like shadows. And, holding Sultan's hand, Atabeg would take it all in with his enormous eyes.

One day Maulana sat down in front of the Kislak, the winter home of the tribes, and asked, 'Do any of you know the meaning of the word Turk?'

— No, Maulana, said Sultan.

— Words are not born without reason. They pass through the uterine passage of a deep mystery. Turk. How magnificent! Have you never felt a thrill uttering this word, Hussam? All that is beautiful is Turk. The ashiq, for instance, the lover. Or take the inhabitants of paradise, they're Turks too.

When the tribes rolled up their tents and began their journey back to the mountains, everyone knew that it was time for new leaves and flowers to sprout on plants. Spring, the messenger of Jannat, was at hand. Dressed in garments of leaves, he was on his way from the blue home of heaven. Then it would start raining. The sky would be covered in thick black clouds. Maulana used to say, those clouds are born in oceans of love to climb to the sky. The more the clouds weep, the more it rains, and the more the gardens smile. The lover's tears also take us towards divine love, Hussam. The embrace of sunshine and rain will reveal our hearts. Rain is the compassion of our lives, Hussam.

Maulana's book of poetry, *Divan-e Shams*, was full of hymns of praise to spring. He observed the marriage between the light of the earth and the light of the sky with the wonder of a child. Walking along the paths of Meram, he was engrossed in the sounds of the whirlpool. 'Do you get a message from the sound of the water, Hussam?' he whispered.

— What message, Maulana?

— The desire to go back home. This is not our home, Hussam. Where did we come from? That's where we must go back.

The nightingale sings from the treetops throughout spring, the call of the cuckoo can be heard. Cuckoo, cuckoo . . . Where, where? Surely the memory of the first day is hidden in the dance manifesting itself through trees and leaves and flowers? Human beings had not yet been born. It was to this non-existence that he had said, 'I am your Lord.' Maulana felt that these words of Allah's were actually the bandish, the melodic line, of his music, and that the eternal dance of life began on hearing this melody.

The beginning of life was in the cosmic dance, my learned readers. The boughs and leaves and flowers start dancing when the spring breeze brushes past them. Walking along the paths of Meram, Maulana would dance too, his favourite dance, the whirling dance, the Sama. Sometimes he spoke incessantly, 'I feel spring is an extraordinary tailor. Indefatigably stitching different kinds of green brocade clothes. Tell me, Sultan, don't you think the tulip bathes in blood like a martyr before revealing itself to us? Do you know the story of the birth of the rose, Thereanos? When Muhammad was on his way to paradise, riding Buraq, the beads of perspiration from his body fell to earth and gave birth to roses. It is the fragrance of the Prophet's body that the rose delivers to us.

Maulana believed that all our thoughts and deeds are like a garden bedecked by spring. I am tempted to read one of his sayings from *Fihi ma Fihi, It Is What It Is*. Maulana says, 'If you speak well of others, it will come back to you as praise for you. If you plant roses and fragrant plants around your house, you will see them all the time, and feel as though you are in heaven. If you speak well of someone they will become your friend; to think of them will be to think of a dear friend. And the rose, the rose bed, and fragrance are the dearest of friends. If you have the constant company of roses, will you ever seek out wild animals in the dense forest?'

It is in spring that bees fly about in Konya's gardens, making wax and honey in their hives. Maulana used to say, 'Each of these bees is a dervish, Hussam. They bring nectar and light to the world just as dervishes do.'

Strolling in Hussam's garden, he stopped at the sight of a

peacock with its tail spread out. Glancing at his followers, he said, 'Who but the peacock can offer such beauty to its lover? Look, Sultan, how his neck is swollen with pride, how it pulses. If this isn't spring, what is?'

— But where is the room for pride in Allah's world, Maulana?

— Some forms of pride are not arrogance but joy. The joy of expressing oneself. The peacock had thought this way too once upon a time. That fanning his tail was a display of pride. Was he demeaning Allah? Wracked by remorse, he tore out the feathers in his tail with his beak. A dervish who was passing burst out in protest, saying, 'What are you doing, peacock?'

— I do not wish to keep my false pride on my body anymore, said the peacock.

The dervish smiled. 'Did you create the beauty of your plumage? This is the Lord's gift. You do not have the right to destroy this beauty. Don't you know that it is your feather which is used to mark the page in the Quran?'

The children start playing again when spring arrives. The long winter has passed in imprisonment in a small room. Now it is time for liberation through the joy of playing. Play as much as you want, roll in the dust, you can even forget the way back home. Only then are you a true companion of spring. In his Masnavi Maulana has written of a shaikh who lost himself playing with children all day. Everyone knew there was no one more learned than him in the city, that he knew the answer to every question.

But he used to hide behind the passion of playing with children. Someone had asked, 'How can a learned man like you spend your time in frolic with children? This is not befitting of you, Shaikh.'

— Do you think you know better than I what suits me or not? Some say, be a lawyer, some say, be a religious scholar. How much do I know? And what I do know has nothing to do with law or religion. You see, I am a field of cane, but I'm savouring the cane sugar at the same time. I don't care whether people believe that I'm learned. You'll never understand the joy of playing all day.

My wise readers, Shams of Tabriz took Maulana into this very joy of sport. The celestial music of the flute played in the empty house of literature, along with the rhythm of drums. The Sama began, a whirling dance linking the earth and the sky. The Sun of Tabriz brought spring into Maulana's life.

One night, when the dancing had ended in the early hours of the morning, Maulana sent for Hussam and said, 'Write down, Hussam . . .

> *Only music day and night*
> *Calm and bright is the melody*
> *Of the flute. When this melody is wiped out*
> *So are we.*

FIFTEEN

It was the height of winter in Konya, but still spring had arrived. Shamsuddin, the Sun of Tabriz, had risen in Maulana's life. Shams knew that he had been born in the house of Aftab, the sunlight, which was why his eyes had been fixed on the sun since birth. One day he told Hussam, laughing, 'Someone asked me, what can you tell us about the moon? Speak about Mars, too. I said, I'm not meant to know all this. Does the sun know that there is something called the moon in the cosmos? The moon and the planets and the stars are all helpless before the sun. Anyone can gaze at the moon, but how many people have that ability when it comes to the sun, Hussam? There was the Sisphur. It didn't drown even in an ocean, but it was burnt in a fire. There are very few birds that neither drown in the water nor burn in a fire.'

— You are that bird, Hussam said.

— No, Hussam. I am merely a pigeon, flying about everywhere. Though I have now been imprisoned in Maulana's cage. But then, you know, some bonds mean freedom. Do you ever feel that way, Hussam? I am complete in you. This skin, blood, bones, marrow, mind, soul . . . all, all of it is you. There is no question of belief or scepticism. This existence is your existence. This is the way I have come to Maulana.

It was like a bright morning dawning after a night of snowstorms and rain. Maulana was playing the rubab in the library. A sight such as this had been beyond the imagination even a short while ago. The whispers in Konya's homes and streets about his transformation grew louder. Would Maulana repudiate Islam, then? What was this path he had chosen? He immersed himself in dance and song and music all day long. Didn't he know that all this was forbidden in Islam? He even forgot to offer the namaz at times, and didn't answer people's questions. Had he forgotten that he was Maulana-e Buzurg Bahauddin's son? How many believers, how many learned men, were there like him in the world? Imagine him falling into the hands of a wandering dervish and giving himself up to singing and dancing.

Maulana spent his entire day with Shams in the kitab khanah. He met almost no one, either from his home or from elsewhere. Only Sultan Walad, Hussam and Thereanos had the right to visit them. Musicians who played the rubab or the lute, the ney or the flute, and the kadam or the drums were allowed in too. Moinuddin Sulaiman and his wife Gurcu Khatun were also occasional visitors. I must tell you a little history here. In 1214 AD, after conquering Anatolia, the Mongols installed Sultan Ghiasuddin's son Ruknuddin on the throne. But he was a mere puppet, with the administration actually still in the hands of Moinuddin Sulaiman.

One evening, Moinuddin Sulaiman and his wife Gurcu Khatun were visiting Maulana and Shams. The finest rubab player of Konya had begun his music. Swaying in time with the music, Maulana rose to his feet a little later. Shams looked at him intently. Maulana held his hands out to Sultan and Hussam. Both of them stood up. Taking their hands, Maulana began to dance. And as he did, he recited:

> *Dance, now that you've been torn apart*
> *Dance, now that you've ripped the bandage off*
> *Dance in the middle of the battle*
> *Dance within your blood*
> *Dance, now that you're a free soul*

When the dance had ended, Moinuddin said, 'Why does the rubab make you so restless, Maulana?'

After a pause Maulana said with a smile, 'I hear the doors of paradise opening.'

— But I'm not transported to your delight. I have no wish to dance.

— Perhaps you hear the doors of paradise closing.

Shams shouted, 'Khamosh! Why do these Sultans and their acolytes still visit you?'

— What do you mean? Moinuddin jumped to his feet, trembling with rage. — You dare insult me through the words of this qalandar, Maulana?

Maulana said placidly, 'My friend has not insulted you.'

— Then what is the meaning of what he said?

Turning to Sultan, Maulana said, 'Explain what it means, Sultan.'

— What can I say, Maulana?

— Then why are you with me? Leave me and go.

— Am I supposed to say everything, Maulana?

Maulana smiled. — Everything. You, I, Hussam, Thereanos, we don't fear anyone anymore. Looking at Shams, he said, 'The sun is with us, Sultan. Whom should we fear? Should we fear Sultan Ruknuddin? Or even Parwana Moinuddin?' Maulana burst into laughter. No one had seen him laugh this way before.

Touching Maulana's feet, Moinuddin said, 'Are you well, Maulana?'

Embracing Moinuddin, Maulana recited:

> *We have barrels brimming with wine, but no goblets*
> *What a perfect arrangement this is, every morning*
> *We brighten, and our glow radiates in the evening too*
> *They say we have no future, and they're right.*
> *What a perfect arrangement this is for us.*

Shamsuddin applauded. 'Magnificent! Shall I tell a story then, Maulana?'

— Tell us.

Clearing his throat, Shams began, 'A long time ago, there were two friends who lived together, and couldn't bear to be parted. One day they went to a shaikh to listen to a story.'

— A story? Hussam asked.

— Why not? Shams smiled too. — A story is no small thing, Hussam. This world of ours was made by weaving stories together. These two friends were addicted to stories.

— And then?

— The shaikh told them a story.

— What story?

— A story about two other friends. They had also been to a shaikh for a story. Before beginning, the shaikh asked them many questions and then said, 'How long have you two been friends?'

— Many years, huzoor.

— How many years?

— Nearly forty. The other friend said.

— That's a long time. You've never quarrelled?

— Never, said the first friend with a smile.

— That means both of you are living a life of pretence. You must have irked each other sometimes, didn't you?

— Yes, huzoor.

— But you didn't dare tell each other out of fear.

— Yes, huzoor.

— There's no need to keep such friendships alive. You can't build a friendship on deception. You were never friends, you only flattered each other.

After a pause Shams said, 'I told Maulana the very first day, all hypocrisy has to be eliminated. You must seek more solitude. Truth does not live in a crowd of people. When I'm on my own, it's my business when I shall shit or fart or piss. If you cannot be alone, when will you get rid of your impurities? Get rid of all the gatekeepers from your life. Most of those who come into your life under the guise of friends are actually gatekeepers. They won't let you go anywhere near the truth.' Shams laughed. 'Moinuddin sahib here is a gatekeeper too.'

'Your friend is insulting me again, Maulana,' muttered Moinuddin.

Maulana bowed his head. 'I beg your pardon, Parwana. But Shaikh has not insulted you.'

— Then what does he mean?

Looking at Sultan, Maulana said, 'You tell him, Sultan.'

Kneeling as though he was praying, Sultan Walad began, 'What I am telling all of you now is what Maulana Rumi told me once. He had said, "Don't rub shoulders with navabs and sultans. These powerful people eventually turn into dragons. Those who converse with them, become their friends or accept their wealth all begin to talk like them on the dragon's wishes. They become preachers of the dragons' credo, losing all power to question them. And that is when a spiritual crisis erupts. The closer you get to dragons, the more you will deviate from the true path. The more you are attracted to worldly things, the more love will slip through your fingers."'

Turning to Maulana, Moinuddin said, 'Do you mistrust me, Maulana?'

— No, but I do not trust your throne.

— The throne is inanimate, Maulana.

— Who says that? Maulana smiled. — Every throne

in the world is bloodthirsty, Parwana. Every throne is an unfulfilled soul.

— I respect you, Maulana.

— But your throne and my rug are far apart.

— You can close the distance easily.

— It can't be done. I am travelling a different road, Parwana. It is a path of poetry, of music, of dance, of beauty.

— I love all this too, Maulana.

— I know, Maulana smiled. — But none of this holds any value for the state. The state cannot proceed except through the route of violence. Nor can you. Murder or be murdered—you do not have the power to escape this fate. I am telling you today that the same Mongols who have vested so much power in you today will be responsible for your death in the future.

Gurcu Khatun shrieked, 'What are you saying, Maulana?'

— Man himself will curb the power of man. It is a spiritual battle to the end. Until it occurs there is no salvation for the world. Parwana . . .

— Yes, Maulana?

— I could have confronted you as a rebel.

— What are you saying, Maulana?

— You are dancing to the tune of the Mongols.

— It is my duty to maintain peace in this city, Maulana.

— Peace? This is a city of the dead. What need does it have for peace? The sword and blood are not my path. Will you join us on our road?

— Which road?

— Singing and music and dance.

— Who will protect the city?

— The people of Konya themselves.

— There will be chaos, Maulana.

— In that case, goodbye. Maulana rose to his feet. — We wish to be left in peace now. Let not the slightest whiff of power enter this room, Sultan.

Without another word, Moinuddin Suleiman and Gurcu Khatun touched Maulana's feet and left.

A few days later, Maulana spoke silently once more against power. That day Amir Jalaluddin, a rich man, had opened a madrassa named after himself in Konya. Maulana arrived with Shams and several disciples for the inauguration. Shams was asked to sit where people took their shoes off, where ordinary citizens sat. He was not Maulana, he was only an ordinary ascetic. Maulana was asked what the seating arrangements should be. Smiling at the question, he said, 'The Maulvis should find room in the centre. The Sufis will sit in the corners. The lover will sit by his lover.'

'Then sit at the centre,' said Amir Jalaluddin.

— But I'm no Maulvi.

— What are you saying, Maulana!

Without another word Maulana Rumi took his seat next to Shams. The hostility to Shams that had been gathering in Konya came to the forefront after the inauguration. Who was this aged dervish who was misleading Maulana? Didn't Maulana know where his seat should be? Had he gone insane?

Many years later, Shams had melted into the wind by then, Maulana stopped at a scene on a road in Konya, where he had been walking with Sultan and Hussam. A she-dog was gnawing on a bone while suckling her puppies. Maulana watched their frolic.

— What is it, Maulana? Why did you stop? asked Sultan.

— Don't any of you have eyes, Sultan? Do you only orbit around me all the time? Look at the world. You might just find me there.

— Tell us what we are unable to see, said Hussam.

— Why shouldn't you be able to see, Hussam? The world can be seen easily enough. But all of you weave a web of explanations and confuse everything. I was once a frog in the same well too. Can explanations offer anything at all? All that we get is on the shorelines of dreams. Do you know who this she-dog is, Sultan?

— No, who is she?

— Mother Mary. Ameen. The little puppies cannot eat solid bones, so their mother is doing it for them. And the babies are drinking her milk. The bone will make fresh milk in her body, which the puppies will drink tomorrow. I know that there are many questions in your mind about my sunlight. What Shaikh used to tell us was like that bone, which you could not digest. I chewed and digested the bone, and all of you drank my milk.

Shams's enemies in Konya were multiplying by the day. What sorcery had this doddering dervish used to captivate Maulana? Unless the infidel was driven out of Konya,

Maulana could not be saved. Another of Maulana's sons, Alauddin, had disliked Shams from the beginning. He had even told Sultan Walad as much, but the dutiful son had dismissed his brother's complaints. Barging into the library in Maulana's absence one day, Alauddin told Shams, 'Leave this building at once.'

— Why? Shams smiled.
— Because I say so.
— Who are you? Are you worthy of talking to me?
— I shall kill you.
Shams laughed loudly. — Pull out your weapon. Where is it? Bring it out.

Unable to stand his ground in the face of Shams's words and his laughter, Alauddin ran away. When Maulana returned home, he sent for Alauddin and said, 'Don't try this ever again, Ala. He is here on my wish, you cannot be his enemy.'

— Will you answer a question?
— What is it?
— Whom do you belong to? To us or to this qalandar?
— To the Sun of Tabriz.
— Are you sure, Maulana?
— I'm absolutely certain.
— What does he have?
— Be civil, Ala. You do not know him at all.
— I don't want to.
— Then stay away.
— Will you not be at our side?
— I will, Ala. I am with all of you. But a time comes

when I have to leave everyone. Do you know why? Because I will come back again. Shaikh Shamsuddin is so much older and wiser. Is it right to insult him?

— He has taken you away from us.

Maulana smiled. 'Listen to me, Ala, no one can take a person away from anyone. Nor have I gone away from all of you. If I ever do, it will be on my own compulsion. You cannot count the number of creatures lurking inside a man. There's a rat, there's a bird too. Don't be the rat. Try to be the bird.'

The pigeon flew away four hundred and sixty-eight days after being seen for the first time. One morning Maulana discovered that Shams was not by his side. He wasn't to be found anywhere even after searching across the length and breadth of Konya. Maulana sat alone in his library. Evening fell, enveloping the room in darkness. He didn't allow the lamps to be lit. Kira came in, sitting opposite Maulana for a long time, but he didn't utter a single word.

Very late at night Maulana went out of the room and called out, 'Hussam . . .'

— Yes, Maulana?

— Come to my room.

Holding Hussam's hands tightly, Maulana said, 'Where has he gone, Hussam?'

— I don't know, Maulana.

— He didn't tell you either? Maulana broke down in tears. — Whom will I live with, Hussam?

Hussam could not answer. Sometime later Maulana began to murmur:

Deep in this new love, let there be death
Your road lies elsewhere
Be the sky
Take an axe to the prison walls. Escape
Emerge like a life born suddenly out of colour
Now, at once
You are shrouded in dense clouds
Run away in secret. Die
And be calm. Tranquillity proves
That you are dead
You had an old life
Running away desperately from silence
Wordless, the full moon
Has just been revealed.

Maulana died once that night. The death before death which hundreds of storytellers in this world have talked of.

SIXTEEN

Everyone had expected Maulana Rumi to return to his former life as a teacher after Shams's departure. A glow of happiness spread across the faces of his students and disciples. But Maulana withdrew himself even more. He spent all his time in the library, without meeting anyone. He asked for all the musical instruments to be removed. No lamps were lit when darkness fell. Despite the extreme cold he often stood stock still in the veranda all night.

A year passed this way. There was no more dancing at Maulana's house, he did not send for Hussam anymore to dictate his poetry.

Sultan described Shams to everyone who came to Konya, asking them whether they had seen the fakir anywhere. Enquiring after his whereabouts became Sultan's principal activity during the day. Atabeg was his constant companion. Sultan knew that his father was going through intense anguish because of Shams's disappearance. Shams would have to be brought back if Maulana was to be saved.

My learned readers, it was during this period of Shams's

disappearance that Maulana Rumi was being cooked in the Lord's kitchen. Don't be surprised to hear this. The kitchen and the process of cooking are both connected with our story. To the Shaikh every disciple was a pea, and he, the cook. The cook at Maulana's house was Ahim Baz, whose grave you can see if you ever visit Konya. Maulana loved him very much, often going into the kitchen to watch him cook. But he did not eat most of the things the cook made. He would ask Ahim Baz, 'Where did you import this aroma from, Ahim bhai?'

— I only present what the Lord sends, Maulana.

— Does the Lord talk to you?

— He does.

— What does he tell you?

— I don't understand any of it, Maulana. The Lord only talks through my hands. He mixes the spices, stirs the pot, sometimes I even hear him tasting what I've made. That's when I know the food is ready.

Listen closely to the story about peas that Maulana wrote in his Masnavi, learned readers. It's an amusing qissa. The peas had been put in the pot to be boiled. How could they stand so much heat? They tried to leap out.

One of the peas asked the cook, 'What are you trying to do with us?'

Rapping the pea with her ladle, she said, 'Don't you try to jump out. Do you think I'm trying to torture you?

— It hurts a lot, wailed the pea.

Smiling, the cook said, 'You have to bear it. After this I'll fry you in spices. Can you imagine the taste? All that water you fattened yourselves on in the garden during the rains—what was it in aid of? So that I could cook you, what else. And then everyone will relish eating you. That's how men will grow sperm in their bodies. And there will be new people in the world.'

The pea smiled too. 'Cook me even better, then.'

— That's just what I want to do, said the cook. — I was like you once. Then I was cooked. So many pure souls ate me. Only then was I born as a cook myself. You won't understand right now what joy it is, pea.

Maulana sent for Sultan and Hussam one morning. Putting his hands on their shoulders, he said, 'I want to go out today.'

— You'll go out?

— Sultan, I can tell that Shams will return. I am certain he will.

— We have not yet received any news of him, said Hussam.

— There *will* be news. There can be no alternative.

When they arrived at Konya's market Maulana told Sultan, 'I want some irmik halva today, Sultan.'

— You? Sultan looked at his father in surprise. Maulana had fasted often during this past year, not even touching any of his favourite foods. He was asking for irmik halva after a long time.

Maulana smiled to himself as he ate.

'What are you thinking of, Maulana?' asked Hussam.

— Of Shaikh Bahauddin.

— Did Maulana-e Buzurg say anything about halva? Sultan asked with a surge of paternal affection as he watched Maulana eat his halva.

— No, Sultan. He had once said, 'I've eaten a lot throughout my life. I can see so much bread and water in my stomach.' Allah says, 'The water and the bread and fruit all sing my praises from your belly.' We have come into this world as raw vegetables and raw meat, Sultan. We look beautiful at that stage. But there will be no release for us till we have been cooked and transferred into people's stomachs. We'll have to die many times before we die, for only then can we reach our companion.

Suddenly Maulana rose to his feet, still eating. A rhythmic sound was floating in from the distance. Maulana followed it back towards its source, stopping in front of a particular shop in the goldsmiths' section in the market. A hammer was falling on gold plates to its own distinctive beat. Like drums. Maulana felt that the flute had struck up a tune too. He stood still for some time. And then the whirling dance began. The people in Konya's market froze. The goldsmith kept hammering the gold plate in time with Maulana's dance, so that the rhythm was not destroyed.

This was how Maulana met the goldsmith Salauddin Zarkub for the first time in the bazaars of Konya. It is said that Salauddin danced that day with Maulana too. Then who had played the beat of the hammer on the gold plate? We do not have the answers, learned readers. It is all the will of God.

Salauddin is supposed to have been born in a village

named Kamil, quite some distance from Konya. The son of a fisherman, he had never been educated. Trying to make a fortune in Konya, he began working with a goldsmith, eventually opening his own modest establishment. Although he met Maulana late in life, Salauddin was also a student of Burhanuddin's.

When the dance ended Maulana clasped Salauddin to his breast. After this Salauddin became Maulana's intimate friend and disciple. Maulana would often visit Salauddin's shop, losing himself in the rhythms of the gold plates being hammered. Salauddin was a reticent man, who could not even express himself properly. But Maulana loved his silent company. He had once told Sultan, 'After the Sun of Tabriz, Salauddin is the moon of my life.' And Hussamuddin Chalabi, his star.

One day Sultan became acquainted with a merchant who had come from Damascus. When he heard Shams being described by Sultan, he said, 'I've seen this sage. Spoken to him too.'

— Where?

— In Damascus.

— What was he doing when you saw him? Was it in a mosque?

— No. A new inn was being constructed. That was where I saw the old man. He was bearing stones on his head. I saw him several times afterwards, reading the Quran to the children of the poor on the street. One day I asked him, 'Who are you?' He looked at me for a while and then answered, 'A pigeon.'

— A pigeon?
— You know what a bird is, don't you?
— But you must have a name.
— Why do you need to know it?
— You seem to be a wise man.
— A wise man? He began to laugh. — What use is wisdom? Let me tell you a story then. A wise man once boarded a boat to cross a river. The boatman began to sing as he rowed. This accomplished individual had his nose buried in a book. A little later he shouted at the boatman, 'Stop singing. I can't read.' The boatman was poor and unread, he fell silent, as the poor always have to. The genius asked, 'Have you ever read a book?' 'No, huzoor, answered the boatman diffidently.' The know-all laughed contemptuously, saying, 'You have lost half of your life.' The boat moved on, the boatman rowing in silence, the genius reading. Suddenly the skies darkened, and a storm was whipped up. The waters began to seethe, the boat began to heave. The know-all was frozen with fear. 'You know how to swim, don't you, huzoor,' said the boatman. Speechless with terror at the violence of the storm, the wise man could barely stammer, 'No.' Even the poor have their day. What else is the Lord here for? Laughing, the boatman said, 'Then you'll lose your entire life, huzoor.' This is the plight of geniuses. They don't even realize how their entire life has been wiped out while they're reading their books.

— Did he say anything more?
— No, he walked off as soon as he had finished the story. A frail old man, but how fiercely he walked.

— He's the sun, said Sultan.

— What do you mean? The merchant looked at Sultan in astonishment.

— The Sun of Tabriz. His name is Shamsuddin.

— The sun or the moon or whatever you may call him, he's a crazy old man. But why are you looking for him?

— Because he is our sustenance. Our wine and our bread.

The merchant laughed. — What you say makes no sense either.

Hussam had been listening in silence. Now he said, 'Listen to a story then.'

— Another story?

Hussam smiled. 'The entire world, and even whatever lies outside it, is a story. The Lord has written all our stories with his own quill.'

— Let's hear it, then.

Taking the merchant's arm, Sultan said, 'But first come and have some hanim gobegi. You're a guest of Konya's, it is our duty to look after you.

— What's hanim gobegi?

— It's a marvellous pastry. The name means a woman's navel. You won't get this famous sweet of Turkistan anywhere else in the world.

The merchant listened to Hussam's story as he ate a woman's navel at a sweetmeat shop.

Hussam began the story he had heard from Maulana.
— There was a philosopher who did not believe in the existence of Allah. One day he fell severely ill and was forced to visit the doctor. The doctor was a very devout

man who believed that the world runs according to the wishes of the Lord. Examining the philosopher, he asked, 'What do you want?'

— I want to regain my health, said the philosopher.

— Hmm . . . said the doctor, looking grave. — Do you know what health looks like? I can restore it to you if you do.

The philosopher said in surprise, 'Can it be seen? How can I tell you what it looks like?'

The doctor smiled. 'How can you want something if you don't know what it looks like?'

The philosopher said in agitation, 'It's true I cannot explain it. But you can understand what health is when you see a healthy person. I have lost the energy of a healthy man.'

— But I was asking about health.

The philosopher said grimly, 'How can I describe what cannot be seen?'

— But still you believe in the existence of health?

— Of course. How can people be healthy otherwise?

The doctor burst into laughter. Shaking with rage, the philosopher asked, 'Are you insane?'

— What if I am? The doctor was still laughing to himself. Then let me ask you a question.

— What is it?

— You cannot see health, but you believe in its existence. Then why don't you believe in the existence of the Lord even if you cannot see him?

The philosopher said loftily, 'It's a philosophical

question, hakim sahib, you won't get it.'

— Philosophy that has no relationship with common sense is not worth its name. Let me ask you one more question.

— All right.

— You've seen the fountains at inns, haven't you? Some of the spouts are made like humans, some like birds. Water flows from their mouths. Now water cannot emerge from the mouths of statues. Where does it come from?

— The source of the water lies elsewhere, smiled the philosopher.

— Yes. And the source isn't visible. All we can see is the fleeting flow from the fountain. But does the source not exist only because we do not see it?

The merchant was listening open-mouthed to Hussam's story. When Hussam stopped he practically shrieked, 'Both of you are very mysterious people. Are you magicians?'

'Would you like another woman's navel?' asked Sultan with a smile.

— Not a bad idea. The merchant's face brightened. 'Far more delicious than an actual woman's navel.'

— No, my friend, said Hussam, smiling. — The taste of a flesh-and-blood woman's navel is indescribable. Every woman's navel has a unique taste, but all hanim gobegi tastes the same. Do you know why?

— Why? The merchant looked at him in surprise.

— Hanim gobegi is made by humans. And a woman's navel, by the Lord. Its flavour and aroma are beyond description.

Coming out of the sweetmeat shop into the market, Sultan told the merchant, 'Will you honour a request?'

— Of course. I like you very much.

— Will you meet Maulana Rumi?

— Who is he?

— My father. The greatest scholar and spiritual soul in the city. All of us are his pupils.

— What do I have to gain by meeting him?

— Nothing at all. The benefit will be all his. Shaikh Shamsuddin is a part of his soul. Ever since he left, Maulana has been like a tree struck down in a storm. He will be very happy to hear you talk of Shaikh.

— That's not a difficult request. The merchant smiled. If it makes a person happy to hear something, it is our duty to say it.

— That's noble of you.

— Not at all. I've travelled all over ever since I was a boy, all in search of money. Not that I haven't amassed a good deal already. But the joy of returning home is special. Now that I'm over fifty, I've realized that happiness is the main thing.

Evening was descending on Konya. Maulana was standing outside his front door. 'Who is he?' he asked, pointing to the stranger accompanying Sultan and Hussam.

— He has seen Shams of Tabriz, Maulana.

— Where? Where has he seen him, Sultan? Maulana gripped his son's arm.

Maulana listened to the merchant's account in his empty

library. Sometimes his face shone with eagerness, at other times anxiety cast a shadow on his eyes, followed by tears of despair. There was a constant play of light and shade on his expression. As soon as the merchant finished his story Maulana took his hands. 'Who are you? What is your name? Where have you come from?'

— My name is Chandradhar Gupta. I'm coming from India.

— India? The land where Shakyamuni was born?

— You know of him?

— I've heard many stories about him that came floating on the wind. Can you tell me more? How many years before Christ was he born?

— I am a mere trader, Maulana. How much do I know about the Buddha? I've heard he reached the status of Buddha only after being reborn many times. The stories have been written in the Jataka tales in the Pali language.

Maulana began to pace up and down. A little later he muttered, 'Search for me elsewhere if you don't find me here. I am waiting for you somewhere, my friend.'

It seemed to Hussam that a planet was trying to break out of its orbit. At that moment Sultan said, 'I want to go to Damascus to bring Shaikh back, Maulana.'

— You'll go, Sultan? But I have to write him a letter first. Why will he come unless I invite him?

Maulana sent four letters to Damascus. Shamsuddin replied too. In one of the letters Maulana had written, 'The light of our hearts, the wish to end all our wishes, our lives have been surrendered to you, do not prolong this separation. Return to our midst soon.'

Shams had responded, 'I have nothing but prayer in my life, Maulana. I no longer have a relationship with anything that is living. Besides you, no other living being exists for me. Wait. I shall return, only for you. Wait. The other name of waiting is prayer. You know this.'

Maulana went mad on receiving this letter. The Sama dances began again. Even on his walks Maulana lost himself in his whirling dances. One day he disrobed entirely while dancing in the market. He started talking to trees, to dogs, as though they were the only ones who could understand him.

Sending for Sultan and Hussam a few days later, Maulana told them, 'You'd better leave for Damascus tomorrow morning, Sultan. Don't travel alone. Let us not lose any more time.'

— Very well, Maulana, said Sultan.

— So much of my life has been wasted, Sultan. Maulana's voice held the dense fog of the Konya winter.

— What are you saying, Maulana?

— I'm right, Hussam. I am renowned the world over as Maulana. I have wasted a great deal of time on this fame. Fame is nothing but shackles of iron. Even those who do not know me claim they love me. There can be no greater misfortune. I don't want to squander the rest of my life, Sultan.

SEVENTEEN

Madinat al-Yasmin. The city of jasmines. I do not know who gave Damascus this poetic name, my learned readers. Do any of you know? The people of Damascus also refer to their city as ash-Sham. The city was built two thousand years before Lord Jesus Christ. I went to Damascus too on my travels, even before reaching Maulana's city, Konya. The walled city has seven gates, their architecture constantly reminding us that Damascus is indeed the city of jasmines. As you know, every beauty has its own distinct fragrance. The gates are beautifully named too—the Bab al-Faradis is the gateway to paradise, the al-Salam is the gateway to peace.

I'm sure you know that after the war at Karbala, the Umayyad Caliph Yazid had brought Imam Husain's severed head to Damascus. It was displayed in the turret of Yazid Manzil for everyone to see. War ends, but its barbarity and cruelty continue to be revealed in different ways. Imam Husain's slow death at Shemr's hands was the most tragic scene from all the wars on earth. But let us not talk of these heartbreaking events and turn back instead to the city of jasmines.

Damascus was redolent with the aroma of knowledge and learning. As you know, Shaikh Bahauddin had sent Maulana to Aleppo and Damascus for a deeper study of religious theory. Maulana lived here for four years. This was where he met the Sufi saint Ibn al-Arabi and Sadruddin Kunai. More important, it was in Damascus that the Sun of Tabriz saw Maulana for the first time, telling himself with a smile, 'He has not been cooked yet.'

I too met an extraordinary individual in Damascus. Taqiuddin bin Tamia. People would throng in thousands to hear him talk at mosques and madrassas. Some of the things he said would enrage scholars. They claimed he was speaking against the religion. He had had to go to jail at least twice. The first time he was imprisoned, he annotated forty volumes of the Quran. But he did not change his ways even after being released. I went to the mosque one Thursday to hear him speak. He climbed down the stairs leading to the prayer platform, and then looked up and said, 'Just like I came down these stairs, Allah too had descended to paradise on Earth.' There was an uproar in the mosque. What sort of assertion was this? Allah had descended to Earth? This was no different from the audacity of the infidel Al Hallaj's saying, 'I am Allah.' Taqiuddin was sent to prison again. Later I heard that he died during imprisonment. Sometimes I think Taqiuddin was actually a ray of light that had burst out of the Sun of Tabriz.

Now we have to go to the forecourt of the Umayyad Masjid, one of the largest mosques in the world. It was originally the Basilica of St John the Baptist. When the Arabs conquered Damascus in 634 AD, the Basilica was converted into a mosque. Searching for Shaikh Shamsuddin on Damascus's roads and in its inns, Sultan and Hussam found him in front of the Umayyad Masjid. He was dressed in a tattered, faded robe, his hair was matted, his beard had turned white. Shamsuddin was talking to a boy, so absorbed that he didn't even look up when Sultan and Hussam appeared.

Clearing his throat, Hussam said, 'Shaikh-e Alam . . .'

— Yes, sir, said Shamsuddin without lifting his head.

— We have come to fetch you.

— Which angels are you? Am I going to Jannat or Dozakh, heaven or hell?

— To Konya. Maulana is waiting for you.

Now Shamsuddin looked at them. To Sultan, his face appeared as calm and bright as the morning light. Raising his arms towards Sultan, Shamsuddin said, 'You've come, Sultan? To fetch me. Oh my Lord, you chose to send a prophet to bring the infidel back.'

— What are you saying?

Shamsuddin jumped to his feet, shouting. — Do you now know who gave birth to you? His seed can only produce prophets.

— What about Alauddin then? Hussam exclaimed.

Shamsuddin began to laugh, rolling with mirth in the forecourt of the mosque. A crowd gathered around him.

Shamsuddin said, 'It's all the Lord's wish. Had it not been for Ala who would have recognized Sultan for who he is? But do not ignore Ala, Hussam. The darkness is also necessary. Do not forget that even the darkness carries Maulana's seed. All the stories in this world are soaked in light as well as darkness, Sultan. You cannot ignore either of them.'

When Shamsuddin had sat up again, Sultan touched his feet, saying, 'We shall spend the night here, and leave early tomorrow morning. Come with us, arrangements have been made for all of us to put up at a khanqah.'

— A rest house? Why?

— Where would you like to stay?

— At an inn. On the road. Why a rest house?

— Would you prefer to stay at a madrassa?

— Why, Sultan? Let me tell you something then. When I came to Damascus, I used to live on the streets or in the forecourts of mosques. I did a few odd jobs and made some money, whereupon I moved into an inn. I would tell stories to merchants every night. Because of these stories, they began to consider me an important person, someone who knew the different roots of religion—it didn't befit me to live at an inn. One day a merchant said, 'You should stay at a rest house.'

— Why?

— You are a holy man.

— Who told you that?

— That's how you appear to us.

— No, I am not worthy of living in a rest house. Do

you know who likes staying at a khanqah? Those who do not want to work for sustenance, those who are afraid to cook. Their time is so precious. It does not suit them to find ways to earn a living or cook their own food. But as for me, I work hard for my money, and I eat off it. You know that building coming up near Bab al-Sharqi? I worked as a brick-carrier there all day. I am not worthy of a khanqah.

Smiling, Sultan said, 'Then we shall sleep on the road. Or we could spend the night on the terrace of the mosque.'

— All in good time. But listen to my story first, Sultan. Another evening, the same merchant told me, 'Then you could stay at the madrassa. A nobleman like you . . .'

— I could have laughed, Sultan, laughed my innards out. I, a nobleman? I had never even allowed the word to enter my life. So I told him I did not have the qualifications to debate in madrassas. There's nothing to debate over what can be understood easily, and if I start talking about myself, everyone will call me an infidel. Yes, an infidel. I talk to Allah every day, if it is wrong to say this, then yes, I am an infidel. But I *shall* talk. I talk to him. And with Maulana. There is no room at the madrassa for either Maulana or me, Sultan.

— Maulana can scarcely hold his impatience anymore for you to arrive.

— I know. But this is my last meeting with him.

— Will you leave again?

— I may be murdered, or I may disappear somewhere forever, I shan't be found again.

— Why not?

— You won't understand now. Let me take you to the graveyard of the poor man. We can spend the night there.

— Very well. Sultan touched Shamsuddin's feet once more.

During their journey from Damascus to Konya, which lasted over a month, Shamsuddin came to love Sultan even more. Sultan, too, felt as though he had been cocooned in the mystic's loving protection from infancy. Shamsuddin had asked Sultan to share his horse, but Sultan hadn't agreed. He walked alongside, holding the reins. Much later Sultan had told Hussam, this journey was the deepest song of joy in his life.

Every night Shaikh Shamsuddin would open his sack of stories in the inns, in the tents pitched by the road, even in the middle of the desert. He stayed up most nights. One day Hussam asked, 'Don't you feel the need to sleep?'

— Maulana stays awake for me every night. How can I sleep, Hussam?

— You'll fall ill.

Shams smiled. 'Is my health more important than Maulana's desire? I am alive only because he is waiting for me, Hussam. What would my life be worth otherwise? My fate would have led me to die somewhere on the road. I am like that boy, Hussam . . .'

— Which boy, asked Sultan.

And then Shams's story began. Hussam would take his stories down in a notebook. I've been told that all these stories recounted by Shams were actually events from his life, which Hussam as well as others noted down. But no one in Konya could lead me to this kitab. When I asked an old man about this in the market at Konya, he said, laughing, 'Mad Shamsuddin's book? It must have been written in air.'

Shams told his story. 'Once upon a time, in my youth, I used to teach the Quran and Hadith. No, not at a madrassa—as you know, I have no faith in madrassas or khanqahs. My little school would be in front of someone's house, or on the roadside. Children from poor families came to study with me. They had no money for madrassas. One of the boys was always entranced as he listened. He refused to leave my side. His parents pleaded with him, but the wretch would not let go of my tail. His parents cried with grief, I locked myself in an entire day, vowing not to meet him anymore. He knocked on the door for a long time before going back.

— You didn't meet him at all?

— No. He ran up a high fever that very night. Unconscious for a few days, he went directly to his grave.

— Didn't you go to see him on his sickbed?

— Of course I did. I told him so many things, but he was unconscious with fever, he heard nothing. For the first time I realized what love is.

After a pause Shams said, 'How is Atabeg, Sultan?'

— He's well. He asks about you every day.

One night Hussam said, 'May I ask you something?'

— Tell me. I know what you're going to ask.

— You do?

— You want to know why I haven't married, why I don't have a family, isn't that so?

— How did you know what I was about to ask?

— You love me so much . . . I can tell which parts of my life you want to know about. Look, Hussam, I do not have the capacity for love. Or else the boy would not have died of fever at eighteen. I have had a terrible life since childhood. I felt like an outsider in Tabriz, where there was no one to call my own. My father seemed to be a stranger who would pounce on me at any moment and thrash me. He used to love me very much, and I used to think he would beat me up and throw me out. I do not have the ability to love, which is why I used to wander about, directionless. Do you know what my nature is like, Hussam? When I am joyful, no sorrow on earth can affect me. A man such as this cannot love. But I do seek love, which is why I am returning to Maulana. He is the boy who died at eighteen. Maulana alone . . . Maulana is the only person in the entire world who is waiting for me.

All his life, Sultan did not forget even the minutest of details of this journey from Damascus to Konya. On the way Shams would often dismount from his horse, losing himself in conversations with people. He would make friends with everyone from peasants to labourers, weavers to masons, thieves and cheats to gamblers. But the moment he saw a priest or a scholar he would run away. Even if they came up to him to talk he would avert his face.

One day Sultan had asked him, 'Why are you so angry with the ulema?'

— Angry? Why should I be angry? I don't even know what a religious scholar is. Have I ever told you what Shaikh Sanai said at the time of his death?

— No.

— Sanai was mumbling at the moment of his death. Unintelligibly. His pupils laid their ears close to his mouth to find out what the master was saying. Sanai was saying, 'I have moved far away from all that I have said all this time—everything I said was meaningless.' Just imagine, Sultan, if Shaikh Sanai could utter such a thing on Judgement Day, who can have anything meaningful to say? Education serves no purpose, Sultan, it is like the frog in the well. You keep licking the sides of the well, but nothing enters your stomach.

On a dark night in the desert, Shaikh Shamsuddin began another story. As he listed, Hussam noticed one particular star in the desert sky becoming increasingly brighter, casting a red light from millions of years ago.

Shams kept talking to himself, as though he were praying. 'I heard about an ancient Jew in Damascus. One day, while reading a book about the saints of the world, he discovered Hazrat Muhammad's name in it. In annoyance he scratched Nabi's name out. On the second day, he found the name back in the book. He smeared ink on it. On the third day, too, he found Hazrat Muhammad's name shining brightly.

— The Lord is merciful, exclaimed Sultan, raising his arms to the sky.

— May Allah shower peace on all of you. Shams

returned to his story. 'The Jew assumed that a prophet must have come to Earth. The book said that he was in Medina. So he set off for Medina. But when he reached, he knew no one there. Seeing him wandering about, one of Nabi's pupils came up to him to ask, whom have you come to see in Medina?

— Take me to Prophet Hazrat Muhammad.

The pupil escorted the old man to Hazrat's mosque. Everyone was overcome with grief there, lamenting with bowed heads. Nabi's inheritor Abu Bakr was present too. The old Jew mistook him for Muhammad. Going up to Abu Bakr, he said, 'This old man has come a long way to see you, Hazrat. I am honoured.'

Everyone broke down in tears. The old man was bewildered, not knowing what he should do.

— And then? Hussam asked eagerly.

— The old man said, 'I am a Jew, I've travelled a long way, and I am a foreigner, moreover, I do not know the rules of Allah's faith. Have I done something wrong? Why are all of you weeping?' Nabi's companion Omar said, 'It is not your fault. The Prophet left this world a week ago. When you mentioned his name we could not contain our tears.' At this the ancient Jew began to tear at his clothes in a frenzy. Abu Bakr himself went up to him to calm him down.

After a silence Shams said, 'See how the desert sky has turned red, Sultan. It's an omen.'

— What omen? Sultan asked in a wavering voice.

— I cannot tell, answered Shams helplessly. — Perhaps

it will take longer to understand. I'd better go on with the story instead. The old Jew said, 'I seek a favour from all of you.'

— Tell us, said Omar.

— I could not see the Prophet. Can you give me one of his cloaks? I will at least feel his touch.

— Only his wife Zohra Bibi can give you his cloak, said Ali. But no one is allowed to visit her.

— Can't we try? the old Jew asked plaintively.

— Come with me.

Pacing up and down, Shams turned to Sultan suddenly. 'Answer a riddle, Sultan.'

— Yes?

— Will he get the Prophet's cloak?

After a pause Sultan said, 'Of course. He will certainly get it.'

— How do you know?

Sultan smiled. 'Your story says as much, Shaikh.'

Shams burst into laughter, twirled a few times, and then stood still to continue, 'They went to Zohra Bibi's house together. When they knocked on the door she asked from within, "Who is it? What do you want?" Abu Bakr explained everything. The door opened. They found Zohra Bibi standing there with the Prophet's cloak. Slowly she said, 'The Prophet had said as much before his death.'

— What did he say, asked Abu Bakr, his head bowed.

— A person will arrive, having travelled a long way. He loves me. He is a very good man. He will not have had the chance to see me. But he will come from so far away, give him this patched cloak of mine. Do not do any harm to him, greet him. Give him a warm welcome.

As he told the story, Shams slumped to the ground, releasing his pent-up tears. Eventually he quietened down and said, 'The old Jew put the cloak on, went to the Prophet's grave and stood there. Death claimed him a little later. If you love someone, Hussam, you are bound to visit them even after their death. Maybe even just for a keepsake. That's no small matter.'

EIGHTEEN

The Sun of Tabriz was returning. The entire house was scrubbed and cleaned, rosewater was sprinkled, fragrant incense was lit. A green flag was hoisted over the front door. Singers and musicians were present. Maulana Rumi stood outside the door, along with his pupils and disciples. And Atabeg, holding Maulana's hand. If I close my eyes I can see the waiting lover, my learned readers, the glow and the anxiety on his face, his eyes lit up with the desire for union and tinged by the agony of separation, as magical as sunset.

Maulana had once said something beautiful. The walls and roof and doors and windows of a house of love are constructed with ghazals and songs. Love was like an oven in whose flames the roasting heart gave off its aroma. Maulana had written in *Divan-e Kabir*:

> 'How is the lover?' someone said
> 'Do not ask,' I answered him
> If you were in my state you would know
> You would also respond to her at once

We do not know what love is, learned readers, but without love the bud of Maulana's life cannot be touched. When Shams had left, Maulana asked love itself one night, 'Tell the truth, who are you?'

A flock of birds were heard beating their wings, the library grew fragrant. Maulana realized love had come on silent footsteps, as a poet was to write hundreds of years later. Again he spoke. 'Show yourself to me, tell me who you are.'

Somewhere a flute began to play a heartbreaking tune. And a voice was heard, 'I am eternal, endless life. I beget life continuously.'

— You are beyond time and place. Where do you live, then?

— In the fire in the heart and in tear-soaked eyes. I live in a house of flames on the bank of the river of tears.

— You're an inhabitant of fire?

— But I am Ranjan, the dyer. I smear saffron on people's faces.

— Where is your Nandini from the poet's *Raktakarabi*?

— Nandini pervades my entire body.

— Your body? Then why is she invisible?

— Because my body is like light, like sound. The human eyes cannot see it. I am a lightning-fast messenger and the lover is my steed. I am the deep red of the tulip. I am the sweetness of laments. Do you want to hear more?

— More . . . tell me more.

— I unveil all that is hidden.

— Unveil me, love.

— You have not been cooked yet.
— When will it start?
— Wait. Wait for the ultimate separation.

Look, learned readers, one of Maulana's students is racing up to him, shouting, 'They're here, Maulana, they're here . . .'

Maulana embraced him when he came closer. 'Where are they now?'

— In the market.
— Did you see Shaikh?
— Yes, Maulana.

Turning to the singers, Rumi said, 'Sing the lyrics of Sanai and Attar.' To the musicians, he said, 'Play the melodies that Shaikh Shamsuddin loves. Yes, the tunes that shepherds play . . .'

The music came alive. The notes of the flute and the rubab mingled. Maulana stood looking at the road, his hands crossed on his chest. The caravan arrived a short while later. Dismounting from his horse, Shams came up to Maulana. They looked at each other for a long time, and then embraced each other, an embrace which wiped out reality. Overwhelmed, Maulana Rumi said:

I never tired of thinking of you, my beloved
Do not deprive me of your compassion

This jar of water, this water-carrier
Must be exhausted with me

A parched fish remains within me
Never given enough water
To quench its thirst

Show me the way to the ocean!
Shatter these half measures
All these tiny containers

All this is sorcery
And mortifying

Let my hut be swept away
By the wave that rose last night
From the depths hidden in my heart

Just like the moon, Yusuf came down into my well
Even if the harvest of my hope has been flooded
What does it matter?

The flames have risen over the tombstone
I seek neither knowledge nor honours
Nor is respect desired

I only want music and this dawn
The warmth of your face on mine

Travellers of heartache are gathering
But I shan't go with them

This is what happens every time
When I have to end a poem

A deep silence envelops me
And I wonder in astonishment
Why I have been pursuing words

Looking into Maulana's eyes, Shams said, 'I could see from Damascus that you have become very lonely, Maulana. I have no weakness for anything in this world, except for you. The Lord alone knows the trouble he has got me into.'

— Come into the house now. Kira has cooked a feast for you, said Maulana with a smile.

— Really? I haven't eaten delicious food in a long time, Maulana.

— Dadajaan! Finally Atabeg took Shams's hand.

— What are you doing here?

— He lives with us, said Maulana.

— That's right, that's right. What's your name?

— Atabeg.

— Yes, Atabeg. A mist has taken over my head these days. There's so much I've forgotten, Maulana.

— You do not wish to remember.

— No, it's not that. He makes us forget because he can. But then forgetting makes life bearable. A wet rag, Maulana, may a wet rag always be with us so that we can wipe out things.

The Sama began that evening. Maulana Rumi's reunion with Shaikh Shamsuddin after fifteen months was certainly a night of Muqabla, the Shaam-e Muqabla.

I must tell you something about the Sama here, learned readers. Just as every star and planet in the universe is strung together on one thread, so too are the Sama and Maulana's life but a single strand. Let the Zikr awaken within us: Allahu Akbar ... There is only one god. We are entering the dream world of the Sama now. It was Maulana himself who had said, 'The Sama is nutrition for the lover's soul, in it is hidden the dream of uniting with Allah.'

What is the Sama? Maulana has explained it himself, let us just listen to him like pupils.

Do you know what the Sama is, Maulana asked in a poem, and answered the question himself. 'Yes'—listening to this sound is the Sama. Listening to him, recollecting him, that's what Sama is. Shed your ego, take yourself out of yourself to reach him, where you can see the lover, where you can discover his nature. Behind the divine curtain you can hear Allah's mysterious conversation. Do any of you know what the Sama is? It is a battle with this flesh-and-blood existence, as though you are writhing like a rooster whose throat has been slit. The Sama is informing you that Yusuf is on his way, the fragrance of his garments is in the air, and Yaqub is on the road to recovery. Do you know what the Sama is? Like Musa, we're swallowing the tricks of the Pharaoh's magicians. Just as Shams of Tabriz bares his heart and sees the divine night, the Sama too comes alive in this way.

After his union with Shams, Maulana would lose himself in a frenzy of dancing, anywhere, anytime. After Maulana's death, Sultan Walad gave the Sama a formal structure in the Maulvi order. It was on his instructions that the practice of dancing the Sama after the afternoon namaz was introduced. It was a ceremonial Sama that I watched in Konya, a performance rather than divine madness. The Samazans, those who take part in the whirling dance, have to go through strict training and hard work. Maulana's divine madness might not exist anymore, but that the Sama makes the material world disappear for some time is no small pleasure.

It begins with a reading of the Naat-e Sharif, praising the Prophet Mohammed. Then the camel-skin drum—the kadam—is heard, its beats containing Allah's instructions at the time of the creation of the universe: Kun, be, come into existence. Then the flute, the Ney, takes over. Do you know what its sound is like? Like Allah breathing.

Then the dancers spread across the arena, whirling to the beat of the drum and the homecoming tune of the flute, on their heads the long white camelhair Sikke, symbolizing the grave, the grave of this soul. Their wide milk-white skirt is named the Tennure, the shroud of the dead. And the black cloak stands for the flesh-and-blood identity, which is why the dancers fling it away before the Sama begins. They start with their arms crossed over their chests, touching their shoulders, conveying the fact that there is only one Allah. Then the dance begins with the arms outstretched, whirling from right to left. The faster they whirl, the closer we get to the truth. The right arm is stretched towards paradise, and the left arm, towards the earth. The right arm brings the Lord's blessings and the left arm passes them on to people in this world of the dead.

Do any of you know what the Sama is? Maulana would say, 'You are Allah's servant, that is the meagre extent of our knowledge. You are on your knees in front of his greatness. Then you traverse the path of divine love to submit to him. Eventually you will reach the objective of this creation—you are the Lord's servant.'

When the Sama ends, when everyone is maddened by the Zikr of 'hu', it appears that the universe is being reborn. Who knows the number of times Maulana Rumi must have seen the birth of the universe in the grips of his divine madness.

Come with me, my learned readers, let us return to the Sama of that night. The wide expanse of the courtyard of Maulana's house had become the setting for a festival. Maulana was dancing with his pupils, Atabeg was dancing too. Shamsuddin sat in a corner, watching the whirling and muttering to himself. Suddenly Hussam thought he heard someone vomiting nearby. He went out of the house, throwing sharp glances everywhere. There were several shadowy figures nearby, one of them vomiting, the others trying to support him. Going a little closer, Hussam recognized Alauddin, it was he who was vomiting. Hussam clasped Ala in his arms at once. — What is it Ala? Are you ill?

— Who are you? Ala snarled, still retching.

— Hussam.

— My father's son. Ala laughed. — I am no one for

Maulana. You are another son of my father's.

— Don't insult Maulana, Ala.

— Who Maulana? He's no Maulana anymore. I don't consider him one.

— Don't drink anymore, Ala. Come home now.

— To see those clowns dancing? You expect me to sit at home for the sake of an old swine and watch them sing and dance like infidels?

— Come with me Ala, I'll help you to bed. You're unwell now.

— Who says I am? Alauddin screamed. — Who says I'm unwell? Is it Maulana or the randy old man?

— I say so.

— You know nothing about me. Extracting a shining dagger from his cummerbund, Ala brandished it in front of Hussam's eyes. — I sharpened this thing today.

— Good for you. Hussam smiled, placing his hand on Ala's shoulder.

— Do you know why?

— I don't want to know.

— I'm determined to kill that old wreck.

— What are you saying, Ala?

— He has hypnotized Maulana. I'm going to bury the old gizzard here in Konya, mark my words. All these people are with me.

Hussam tried to identify Ala's companions. He had seen two or three of them at Maulana's madrassa, but the rest were strangers. Who were these people?

— Let's go home now, Ala.

— No need to worry about me. Go watch the dance. Why are you here? Allah himself will visit today, don't you want to catch a glimpse?

The Sama had ended, everyone had gone home, the courtyard was empty. Entering the library, Hussam found Shamsuddin, Maulana Rumi and Sultan all sunk in thought. Maulana said, 'What is it, Hussam? Where did you go?'

— I was out for a walk.

— You never abandon the Sama. Is something wrong?

— No, Maulana.

— Hussam! Shams roared. — You've just been told about the conspiracy to kill me, haven't you?

— No . . . I . . . I . . .

— Don't you know Shams can see everything, Hussam? Why are you lying, then? It is for Maulana that I have come to Konya for the last time. It is irrelevant to me whether I live or die. The cooking is almost done, whether the cook survives or not is immaterial.

— Hussam . . . Maulana sounded like a river flooding its banks.

— Yes, Maulana?

— I shall go to Salauddin's house with Shaikh tomorrow morning. We shall stay there.

— Why?

— You won't understand. Make the arrangements.

— Very well.

Shams smiled. 'There's no escape, Maulana. The final test is here.'

NINETEEN

Maulana moved into Salauddin's tiny, dilapidated wooden house with Shams. Hussam was a little vexed and disappointed, for he had wanted Maulana to live in his house. He had even told Maulana once, 'My house is your house too, you can live there exactly as you wish to.'

Maulana smiled. 'I know I will lack for no comfort in your house, Hussam. But I need something else now.'

— What do you need, tell me, asked Hussam like an obdurate child.

— I am about to enter the tandoor, Hussam. Only then can the kebab be made.

There was an uproar in Konya again. Maulana Rumi had apparently told everyone that Shams was his lover and the two of them needed to live together by themselves. No one should disturb them. Only Salauddin and Sultan were allowed to visit them—not even Hussam.

But they did not spend forty days together in a locked room, as they had last time. Both Salauddin and Sultan visited Maulana occasionally. The madrassa had reopened, and Maulana even taught there regularly. Shams wandered about alone on the roads now and then.

Hussam alone had noticed some sort of restlessness growing in Maulana. A few days later Maulana once again stopped visiting the madrassa and his own house. He spent all his time in Salauddin's room, staying back alone when Shams went out.

One day Maulana sent for Hussam. Going out for a walk, they stopped at the fields outside the city. Maulana sat down on the road, and so did Hussam, after kissing his feet. Maulana was a silent statue. 'What is it Maulana?' asked Hussam. 'Why are you so worried?'

Taking Hussam's hands in his own, Maulana said helplessly, 'What will I do, Hussam? He wants to leave.'

— Why?

— My work is done, he says.

After a silence Hussam said, 'Can I ask you something, Maulana?'

— Yes.

— I want to know what this unknown fakir has given you.

Maulana smiled. 'Listen to a poem. I composed this in my head last night for my sun:

> *Love and patience are not companions*
> *Logic cannot stem your tears*
> *Madness is the name of a beautiful city*
> *Which none of its inhabitants can tame*

The caravan of life moves on
But no one can hear the bells ringing

He made me listen to a bell, Hussam. Unless he had arrived I would never have known that I am an uprooted man. There are so many things he told me during those forty days, showing me the entire world in that room. The famous prince's story was enacted inside the room.'

— Which prince?

— An Indian prince. His name was Siddharth. He received enlightenment, bodhi, and became a Buddha.

— What's bodhi?

— The knowledge that frees you. The knowledge that says, this is not where your home is. This resonates within me constantly, Hussam, this is not where your home is. Then where is it? What foreign land am I living in? Will death take me home again? My sun says, 'No, there is nothing after death. Look for your home while you're still alive.' How will I look for it? 'Lose yourself in love, let madness overcome you.' Mad for whom? 'For he who created your ancestor, Adam. Your home lies in his formlessness.' But Hussam . . .

— Tell me everything that's on your mind, Maulana.

— Hussam, all I do when I hear all this is to write poetry in my head. As I arrange the words, I feel my home is in this very world, I can touch it, feel it. I cannot bear formlessness, Hussam. Am I an infidel, then? I am still amazed by Kira's loveliness.

— Her beauty is a gift from heaven.

— I know, Hussam. But this is still physical, bodily desire. This curtain must be torn apart one day. Only then will I be able to glimpse Lord Jesus Christ. But see, I'm still trapped in the body of a fat donkey. When will I grow lean and become Jesus's donkey? I have been waging this battle for a long time. Who will win—the donkey or I? Let me tell you a story, Hussam.

— Tell me.

— This is the story of a merchant's wife. The merchant travelled from one country to another on business. His wife stayed at home with maids and servants. Her principal maid was involved in a strange act. Every day she would go into the cattle shed to copulate with a donkey. You have seen the size of a donkey's penis, haven't you, Hussam? How can a woman survive with such a huge organ in her vagina? The maid had devised an ingenious method. She would induce the donkey to insert his penis into the frayed husk of a gourd, and then press the gourd to her own vagina, so that only a portion of the organ entered her. The maid achieved sexual satisfaction in this way. As the days passed, the donkey grew thinner and thinner. The merchant's wife was astonished. What was this, why was the donkey turning into skin and bones by the day? She sent for a veterinarian doctor. His examinations revealed nothing. Then the merchant's wife decided to unravel the mystery herself. One day she peeped through the door of the cattle shed to discover the maid lying beneath the donkey, moaning in pleasure.

— Where did you hear this story, Maulana? Hussam

looked at Maulana in surprise. Maulana had never recounted a tale like this before.

— In Aleppo. In the markets of Aleppo.

— And then?

— The merchant's wife began to tremble with arousal at what she was seeing. Is this even possible, she wondered. Then I have the first right. A little later she knocked on the door, whereupon the maid hid the gourd and began to sweep the floor as she opened the door. Sending her out of the house on the pretext of an errand, the merchant's wife locked the door of the cattle shed. She was maddened with desire. Meanwhile the maid mused, 'It wasn't wise of you to push me out, Bibi sahiba. You do not know how to use the gourd, what if you die?'

— And then? Hussam was aroused too.

Maulana laughed. — You feel desire, don't you, Hussam?

— Maulana . . .

— You're human. How can you escape it? In the meantime the merchant's wife's vagina was singing like a nightingale with sexual arousal. Lying beneath the donkey, she pulled it close. At first she felt great pleasure, but as soon as the donkey's organ penetrated her, she could not utter a word, dying at once. Her blood flowed all over the shed. When the maid returned, she found her mistress dead. 'Bibi sahiba, you saw what I was doing,' she told herself. 'But you did not know my secret. You saw the donkey's enormous penis, but not the gourd.' What do you make of this story, Hussam?

Hussam was silent. The story was a conundrum.

Maulana continued, 'We are human beings, Hussam. Do you know what humans are like? Like a donkey with a pair of wings. Whether you will stay in the cattle shed or fly in the sky depends on your wishes and your abilities. You mustn't die because of the donkey—you must control it. Like Lord Jesus Christ's donkey. It grew more and more emaciated by the day. But all our donkeys are fat creatures, bloated with blubber. Allah alone knows when my donkey will become skin and bones, it's all Lord Jesus Christ's will.

— You need rest, Maulana.
— What sort of rest? Maulana smiled.
— Come and live in my house. I shall look after you.
— And my sun?
— He'll come too.

After being silent Maulana said, 'It's not so simple, Hussam. There's something I have thought of. How about bringing Kimia along with my sun?'

— What are you saying? Kimia is a young girl. Shaikh Shamsuddin is forty years older.

— So what, Hussam? If they get married the sun won't be able to leave me anymore.

My learned readers, I have told you about Kimia already. As you can understand now, she was not Al-Mustasimi's daughter. Maulana had adopted this girl from the hills. He loved Kimia very much. He had personally taught her to read the Quran.

Maulana made the proposal to Sultan Walad. Bowing his head, Sultan said, 'Perhaps you do not know, Maulana, that Ala likes Kimia very much.'

— So what?

— Ala and Kimia . . .

— I was wrong to consult you, Sultan. Ala is not worthy of Kimia.

— You consider the old man worthy of her?

— I do. I want the sun to stay with me.

— You'll use Kimia for that purpose?

— Are you arguing with me, Sultan?

— No, Maulana, I have never disobeyed you. But I am saying that this decision is wrong.

— Why?

— You cannot ruin a twenty-year-old girl's life like this.

— Don't you know my sun, Sultan? Are you not aware of his powers?

— But what about Kimia's wishes?

Maulana smiled. 'What wishes can a little girl like her have?'

Grasping Maulana's feet, Sultan said, 'Don't do this, Maulana. You have never harmed anyone. This will cause irreparable damage.'

Maulana said grimly, 'Stand up, Sultan. Arrange for the marriage of Shaikh Shamsuddin and Kimia.'

Sultan stood in silence. Maulana said, 'What you waiting for? Do you have anything else to say?'

— Reconsider your decision, Maulana.

— You do not trust my judgement?

— It's not that. You know Shaikh. He considers himself a pigeon. He told me once, birds never roost in the same place, they fly away from their families to other skies in search of other lives.

Maulana smiled. 'That is why I thought of getting Kimia married to him. I want to tie him down with love, Sultan. Make the arrangements.'

Kira tried to dissuade her husband too, but to no avail.

Smiling at Maulana's proposition, Shamsuddin said with a smile, 'It shall be as you wish, Maulana. I have never been a slave to my own wishes. Whatever I have gathered on the road is the treasure of my devotion.'

Maulana went into the mahalsarai to speak to Kimia. Touching his feet, Kimia said, 'Your wish is my command, Maulana.'

— You've seen Shaikh. He is an old man, much older than . . .

— I don't know Shaikh, I don't know who he is. I know only you. I can lay down my life for you, Maulana.

— What are you saying, Kimia! Could I ever ask for such a thing?

Kimia's words seemed to foreshadow the future. Kimia did lay down her life for Maulana. More of that later. Meanwhile Alauddin was furious at the news. He had had his eyes on her ever since she had started living in Maulana's house. It was his ardent desire that Kimia be his wife one day.

He cornered Sultan Walad outside the house. — Kimia getting married to the old man? Is this true, Bhaijaan?

— It is.

— Has Maulana gone mad?

— Don't talk about Maulana like this, Ala.

— All of you are turning into puppets, Bhaijaan.

— What would you suggest? Sultan smiled.

— Throw the old fool out of the house at once. Or else I shall kill him.

— What are you saying, Ala!

Ala pulled a dagger out of his cummerbund and showed it to Sultan. — You don't know me, Bhaijaan. I have waited a long time. If Kimia gets married to the senile fraud, blood will be shed in Maulana's house.

— Listen to me, Ala, opposing Maulana's wishes would mean none of us is his disciple.

— Yes! Ala laughed loudly. — I am not his disciple, Bhaijaan, I am his son.

— You're walking the path of Iblis, Ala.

Ala was silent for a while. Then he said, 'Iblis too is one of Allah's angels. Wasn't he cast out of heaven only because he did not wish to bow before a man made of clay? But he also managed to extract from Allah the power to live till Judgement Day and lead people astray. As you know, his punishment has been suspended till Judgement Day. But do any of us know when Qayamat will come? I am prepared to be punished. If I can't have Kimia, Bhaijaan, I am prepared for any punishment.'

Kimia was married to the Sun of Tabriz. A short conjugal life. Could it even be called conjugal? Shams and Maulana spent most of their time together, while Kimia stayed in the ladies' chambers. It was said that Maulana often slept alongside Shams and Kimia at night.

Kimia and Shams were married at the end of autumn, and on a freezing winter night that same year, Kimia went missing. Shams was unhappy. How could his wife go out in the evening without seeking his permission? After a great deal of searching Kimia limped back home on her own, bedraggled after a snowstorm.

— Where did you go? Shams snarled.
— To the garden at Meram.
— Alone?
— Yes.
— Why?
— I wanted to go for a walk. Kimia slumped to the ground, unconscious. The best doctors of Konya came, but Kimia died on the third day. For a long time Maulana sat looking at her face, heavy with death. Then he went out to the balcony. Sultan went up to him, saying, 'Shall we arrange for the burial?'
— Yes.

As Sultan was leaving, Maulana called him back. 'Listen, Sultan.'
— Yes?
— I have punished you harshly.
— What do you mean?
— You had to make the arrangements for Kimia's wedding as well as funeral. Maulana started sobbing.

Sultan grasped his feet. — Calm down, Maulana, I'll make all the arrangements.

— Do you know what Kimia told me?
— What?
— I can lay down my life for you. I had never imagined she would lose her life, Sultan. May the Lord forgive me.

Sultan stood next to his father in silence for a long time. Then he said, 'I want to tell you something.'
— Yes?
— Kimia died with peace in her heart, Maulana.
— What do you mean?
— She had gone to the garden at Meram to meet Ala.
— How do you know? Maulana dug his nails into Sultan's shoulder.
— Ala himself told me. Kimia had wanted to meet Ala in private at least once.
— And then?
— Ala spoke to me that night and left this house.
— Where has he gone?
— He's in an inn somewhere. I'm told he's drunk all day. Apparently he has been spotted with hired killers.
— Why? What does he want to do?
— I don't know, Maulana.
— I'm sure you do. Tell me.
— I really don't. I'd better go and make arrangements for the burial.

Kira bathed Kimia with her own hands. Her body was smeared with sandalwood oil, amber and rosewater, and covered in a light brown shroud. Shams and Maulana were present as people prayed for Kimia. At one point Shams said, 'This body, this existence, is the source of agony. As for me, I float on an ocean of joy. Why did you have to introduce this external source of pain to my life, Maulana?'

Maulana smiled. 'We have to die several times before our death, Shaikh.'

Gazing at Kimia, Shams said, 'It is time for me to leave again, Maulana.'

— Very well. But before you do, let us lay Kimia down.

Maulana Rumi's house remained sunk in silence for several days after Kimia's death. One day Maulana sent for Sultan and Hussam and told them, 'I have some things to discuss with you. Let's go to Meram.'

— Meram in this weather? Hussam asked.

Maulana smiled. 'I must test myself. How much can I really bear?'

It kept snowing that afternoon. Sultan and Hussam walked behind a silent Maulana in the gardens of Meram. Maulana called out to them softly, 'Sultan . . . Hussam.'

— Yes?

— I'm a famous Maulana, am I not? Countless students from near and far came to learn from me. Then the Sun of Tabriz took me flying into the sky. How terrifying the world of stars and planets is, what a cruel game of life and death. I could not bear to be in that sky anymore. Kimia's death has brought me crashing down on this world of the dead. I know what love is. With her death Kimia has taught me that if you can love someone even for a day, there's nothing greater. She sacrificed her life for me, she gave up her life for Ala. I remember an old incident. A long time ago, some butchers had captured a female calf and were leading her to the slaughterhouse. Suddenly the calf broke free of the rope and began to run. The butchers chased her, screaming, and the calf ran faster. I was passing that way. Seeing me, the calf stopped. I have no idea why. I caressed its head, its shoulders. She seemed to feel safe with me. The butchers had arrived by then. I begged for the calf's life. The butchers did not slaughter her. But I could not save Kimia, Sultan.

— It's all the Lord's wish, Maulana. Come back home now, said Sultan.

— I am in a quandary, Sultan.

— What is it, Maulana?

— Whom am I bound to? Is it to the one who cannot be seen? Or to the one who is always with me?

— You are bound to both.

Maulana shouted, 'You are my finest progeny, Sultan. Be my master today onwards.'

— Don't embarrass me, huzoor.

Clasping Sultan to his breast, Maulana sobbed, 'You are my heart, my son.'

TWENTY

A harsh winter night. Konya was covered in snow.

Maulana Rumi, Shaikh Shamsuddin, Sultan, Hussam and Thereanos were seated in the library. For a long time they had all been silent, lost in thought, as though waiting for something to happen, for some news to be brought to them.

Suddenly Shams said, 'Would you like to hear the story of Fariduddin Attar, Maulana?'

— Which story?

— The one about the three butterflies.

— Tell us.

— Tonight is the final night of our stories, isn't it, Maulana? Shams smiled.

— If the Lord so wills.

— Three butterflies were flying about in an empty room. A single candle was burning. The first butterfly flew close to the flame and then shot away. So hot, so hot. How could its tender body stand so much heat? Shams began to laugh.

Then he muttered to himself, 'He was undeveloped. How could he bear the heat?'

Sultan began to look around suspiciously.

— What is it, Sultan? Maulana asked.

— I hear footsteps outside.

— You're imagining things, said Shams. 'Now the second butterfly flew up to the flame and singed one of its wings. In agony and fear this butterfly flew away too. Our Maulana was in the same state once. But neither of these two butterflies found out what fire is.'

A voice was heard outside the door. 'Come out, Shaikh Shamsuddin.'

Shams said loudly, 'Just a minute, my friend. Let me tell them about the third butterfly.' Looking at Maulana intently, he said, 'The third butterfly dived into the flames. Who but the burnt butterfly can find out what fire is?'

Sultan and Hussam saw Shams's face losing colour slowly. Maulana's eyes were fixed on his sun.

Shams said, his voice wavering, 'They want to kill me. The murderers are here.'

Maulana did not answer.

Once again the voice was heard. 'Come out at once, Shaikh Shamsuddin.'

Shams got to his feet, his knees trembling, looking at Maulana with fear in his eyes, along with hope for protection.

Maulana was silent. Sultan jumped up, saying, 'Let me see who it is at this hour . . .'

— Sit down, Sultan. Maulana issued a command.

The voice was heard again. 'Are you coming, Shaikh Shamsuddin?'

Shams's eyes reflected the look of a sacrificial cow. Shutting his eyes, Maulana began to recite the Surat ul-Ikhlas, 'Say, Muhammad, he is the only Allah. He is the Eternal Refuge. He neither begets nor is born. He has no equivalent.'

Shams waited no longer, opening the door and going out. A shriek was heard a little later.

Going out, Sultan and Hussam saw fresh blood on the snow. But there was no one to be seen. Shams was nowhere to be found.

There are many mysteries surrounding the last disappearance of Shaikh Shamsuddin, my learned readers. I heard a great deal about this in Konya. Ala was supposed to have had Shams killed by hired assassins, and then thrown into a well. Apparently Maulana broke off all ties with Ala after this. Ala died before Maulana, who was not present at the prayers for him. Many people felt that Sultan was also involved in the conspiracy, which Maulana had not come to know. And the wandering dervishes said that Shaikh Shamsuddin was united with Allah that night—it was the night of Shaikh's urs—his wedding night.

Forty days after the disappearance of the Sun of Tabriz, Maulana Rumi's garments changed. His white turban became grey, his robe was striped black and white. He wore these signs of separation till the day of his death. He even went to Damascus twice or thrice in search of Shams, but no one could give him any news.

One say Hussam told him, 'You needn't go looking for him. We will find him for you.'

Maulana smiled. 'Don't look for him anymore, Hussam. It was I who let him go out that night.'

— Why did you? I was astonished, Maulana. Your silence that night still weighs me down like a rock.

— I know, Hussam. But this parting was necessary. Do you know another word for parting? It's 'cook'. Our parting is cooking me, I am becoming more delicious as I am roasted in its oven. I get the smell of delectable kebabs from my own body. He had become a burden, you know. A heavy burden. He is a dove, who flies constantly from one sky to another. He is a migratory bird. I am a robin or a sparrow. I don't like flying incessantly, I prefer to alight on earth from time to time, I have an urge to peck at grains scattered on the ground. I am distressed, Hussam. I do not understand who I am.

— Don't you want Shaikh to come back?

— I don't, Hussam. During his absence I have realized that he is I. He is inside me, I am inside him. We are not separate.

That night the drums sounded, the weeping of the flute spread across the earth, while Maulana Rumi lost himself in his whirling dance.

The Sama ended late at night. When everyone had left Maulana sent for Hussam. — Get your pen and paper, Hussam. A poem has been born for him.

Hussam prepared to write. Maulana recited:

When the prayers begin after my death
Don't think I'm sad to leave this world
You mustn't cry for me or mourn my going
Don't fall prey to the devil, that would hurt
Never say at the funeral, 'He is leaving'
For this is when I shall be reunited
Do not say 'goodbye' when you lay me down
The grave is but the lid to the meeting in heaven
When you see me lowered, think of rising high
Can the sun or the moon ever be lost?
What you think of as sunset is the sunrise
The grave is not a prison, it frees the soul
Haven't you seen the tree sprout from a seed?
I'm a human seed too, don't you see?
When you close my mouth on this side
It opens at that moment on the other
Let your song echo in the emptiness.

When he had finished, Maulana sat in silence for a long time. Then he said, smiling, 'So he did leave eventually, Hussam? Where did he go? Into what invisibility? Just think, Hussam, how marvellous this disappearance is. He unfurled his wings, broke the cage, and flew away. Like a nightingale desperate for love amidst owls, who flew to the rose garden as soon its fragrance wafted in. Don't grieve, don't weep, be joyous, Hussam. He is manifest everywhere today. Call him the sun of Anatolia.'

Kissing Maulana's feet, Hussam said, 'You are the light of Anatolia.'

Maulana planted a kiss on his forehead. 'My liberation is in light,' he said, quoting a poet from the future.

A few days later he sent for Sultan and Hussam. — I need some rest. And there's something important that has to be done. So I had to take a decision.

— What is it, Maulana? Sultan asked.

— I wish to pass on the responsibility for all my work to the goldsmith Salauddin. I hope the two of you have no objection.

— How can there be any objection once you have stated your wishes, Maulana, Hussam said.

— Salauddin is a very ordinary man, not very well educated. But you won't find a heart like his anywhere in Konya. He is the moon of my life.

— And what is the important thing you spoke of, Maulana? Sultan's eyes were questioning.

— Something quite useless, Sultan. Maulana smiled.

— Useless?

— I have no use for important things.

— What are you saying, Maulana . . .

— Hussam.

— Yes, Maulana.

— Do you have pen and paper?

— I do.

— Then write.

Hussam prepared to write. Maulana recited:

Listen to the mourning of the flute,
The lament of separation in its heart

Since I was uprooted from the bed of reeds
My tunes have only held the grief of men
I just seek the heart that has broken
Into two, I can talk only to this heart
Everyone exiled from their roots dreams
Of returning, of being reunited
I wander all alone in a crowd
I talk with people, make friends too
Still my mystery remains unfathomed
My melody holds the burden of eternity
Neither eyes nor ears can touch it
This body and soul are fused together
But not everyone can enter the soul
The weeping of the flute is not just wind,
It's fire too. Without a fire within,
It's better to die. The desire of the flute
Is love's flame, its warmth inspires wine
The flute befriends lonely, banished men
It draws the curtain away from their heart
Nothing can cure like the tune of the flute
The road ahead is difficult, the flute says so
Writing of the lover's bloodstained heart
Anyone can survive on a single drop of water
Still the fish wants the ocean every day
What the kebab thinks
Is impossible for raw meat to imagine
Break your chains, my child, be free
How long will you remain a slave to gold?
You're trying to capture the sea in a goblet

It can hold things for only a day
Greedy eyes hold no satisfaction
Content oysters give birth to pearls
The lover's clothes are torn off the same way
The madness of love makes him fly
Through the air, but he who is abandoned
By love wanders on empty roads
The wingless bird knows this regret
'How shall I be calm on this lonely night
For my lover casts no light here.'
Love wants its story to be heard
But this sun shall not rise in the mirror
Of your heart. Do you know why we cannot see him?
The mirror is soiled, bring its sparkle back.

This was the poem with which the composition of the Masnavi began, learned readers. Many people term it the Persian Quran. I only call it poetry. It was written in six volumes, strung with the flowers of 25,668 couplets. Maulana would recite the verses, and Hussam would write them down. There was no specific time of day for composing the Masnavi. Maulana would dictate at the madrassa, at the hamam, in Konya's markets. As though it were a tree growing slowly within Maulana, without his knowledge, and now rich with flowers and leaves and fruits. Shamsuddin, the Sun of Tabriz, had planted the seed. Sometimes Maulana recited all night, Hussam would have no opportunity for sleep. After every volume was completed, Hussam would read the verses out to

Maulana, who made corrections as required. The title and introduction to each volume was written in red ink. It was to Hussam that Maulana dedicated this epic in verse.

Our kitab ends here, learned readers. Maulana would recite the introduction to each volume in prose. I wish to read part of the introduction to the fourth volume to end this majlis. Shut your eyes, all of you. If the Lord so wills it, you may be able to hear Maulana's voice.

This is our fourth journey homewards. Home—that is where all our wealth lies. Mystics will be happy to read this book, just as the prairie is pleased by rolls of thunder and signals of rain, just as tired eyes await sleep. The sun is rising, and its light will convey these volumes to our successors. May Allah, who sang all creation into existence, bless all of you. Ameen.

A NOTE ON THE AUTHOR

Rabisankar Bal is a Bangla novelist and short-story writer, with over fifteen novels, five short-story collections, one volume of poetry and one volume of literary essays. Born in 1962, he has been writing for thirty years. His novel *The Biography of Midnight* won the West Bengal government's Sutapa Roychowdhury Memorial Prize. *Dozakhnama*, acknowledged by the late doyen of Bengali literature, Sunil Gangopadhyay, as the finest novel of 2010, won the West Bengal government's Bankimchandra Smriti Puraskar. He has edited a collection of Saadat Hasan Manto's writings translated into Bangla. A journalist by profession, he lives in Kolkata and passionately follows literature, music, painting, and world cinema.

A NOTE ON THE TRANSLATOR

Arunava Sinha translates contemporary and classic Bengali fiction into English. He has seventeen published translations to his name. Born and educated in Kolkata, he lives in New Delhi.